RANDOM HOUSE
CHILDREN'S BOOKS

☞ **W9-AGQ-436**

TITLE:	Marcus Makes a Movie
AUTHOR:	Kevin Hart with Geoff Rodkey
ILLUSTRATOR:	David Cooper
ILLUSTRATIONS:	Black-and-white illustrations
IMPRINT:	Crown Books for Young Readers
PUBLICATION DATE:	June 1, 2021
ISBN:	978-0-593-17914-7
TENTATIVE PRICE:	$16.99 US/$22.99 CAN
GLB ISBN:	978-0-593-17915-4
GLB TENTATIVE PRICE:	$19.99 US/$25.99 CAN
EBOOK ISBN:	978-0-593-17916-1
AUDIO ISBN (CD):	978-0-593-41117-9
AUDIO ISBN (download):	978-0-593-21243-1
PAGES:	208
TRIM SIZE:	5-1/2" x 8-1/4"
AGES:	8–12

Please send any review or mention of this book to:
Random House Children's Books Publicity Department
1745 Broadway, Mail Drop 9-1
New York, NY 10019

rhkidspublicity@penguinrandomhouse.com

What's up, book people???

Kevin Hart here: comedian, actor, producer, entrepreneur ... and now a children's author.

It's not the usual career move. But when I was growing up in North Philly, there weren't a whole lot of kids' books I could see myself in. I want to do my part to put some new faces on your shelves.

Even more, I want to INSPIRE KIDS—especially the kids like me, who didn't have much growing up— to DREAM BIG and work their butts off to make those dreams come true.

When I was coming up, all I heard was NO. *No, you can't. ... No, you're not good enough. ... No, you don't have the right education or know the right people. ...* Blah blah blah. I'm stubborn, so I turned those NOs into fuel. Every time I heard one, it just made me work harder to prove wrong whoever said it.

But not every kid is like that. A lot of them hear NO and believe it. When they do, we ALL lose out. Because there's greatness in them! But if they quit before they even get started, it never has a chance to develop!

I wanted to create a story that'd help those kids believe in themselves by showing them somebody who's just like them, who draws his own road map and then follows it down a long, wild path to success.

The hero of *Marcus Makes a Movie* is a lot like I was growing up. He doesn't have money or connections; he's not a great student or a star athlete. But he's got BIG DREAMS, and he's willing to put in the HARD WORK to make them come true. As Marcus and his partner-in-hustle, Sierra, try to turn his superhero-movie idea into an ACTUAL movie, they hit a ton of roadblocks. And they screw up a LOT. But these kids NEVER QUIT—and by the end of this first story, they've created something they're proud of.

That's only the beginning of their journey. This is the first book in a series I'm cowriting with Geoff Rodkey, the dopest middle-grade author I know. We'll make EVERY kid who reads this book laugh, we'll make MOST of them cry (for real! Chapter 25's going to knock you on your butt, people!)—and if we did our jobs right, we'll inspire some of them to GET OUT THERE AND HUSTLE after their dreams the same way I did.

Enjoy! It's a fun ride! And we're just getting started!

MARCUS
MAKES A MOVIE

KEVIN HART
WITH GEOFF RODKEY

ILLUSTRATED BY DAVID COOPER

CROWN BOOKS FOR YOUNG READERS NEW YORK

All rights reserved. Published in the United States by
Crown Books for Young Readers, an imprint of Random House Children's Books,
a division of Penguin Random House LLC, New York.

Crown and the colophon are registered trademarks of
Penguin Random House LLC.

Visit us on the Web! rhcbooks.com

Educators and librarians, for a variety of teaching tools,
visit us at RHTeachersLibrarians.com

Library of Congress Cataloging-in-Publication Data is available upon request.
ISBN 978-0-593-17914-7 (trade) | ISBN 978-0-593-17915-4 (lib. bdg.) |
ISBN 978-0-593-17916-1 (ebook)

The text of this book is set in 12-point Kievit Slab Pro.
Interior design by Carol Ly

Printed in the United States of America
10 9 8 7 6 5 4 3 2 1
First Edition

To Heaven, Hendrix, Kenzo, and Kaori:

You inspire me so much.
May you have the courage to dream big . . .
the strength to do the hard work it takes
to bring those dreams to life . . .
and the heart to pick yourself up, laugh,
and keep going when you fail.

Your generation can change the world!

CHAPTER 1

THE WORLD'S GREATEST SUPERHERO

Dead Eye wasn't just any old villain.

He was a SUPERvillain! Seven feet tall! Muscles like rocks! With a whole crew of henchmen: the Dead Boyz.

They were marching through Center City, looking for folks to rob.

Junior high was letting out. Kids were everywhere. Dead Eye checked out the crowd.

He spotted this one kid, walking all alone.

Skinny little boy with no muscles. The perfect victim!

Dead Eye came at him. "Empty them pockets, Little Man!" he yelled.

Skinny little kid took off.

Dead Eye and the Boyz chased him all the way down Main Avenue.

Kid's heart was beating like a drum. They were gaining on him!

He ran into Mr. Lee's deli. Hid all the way in the back, behind the potato chip rack.

Dead Eye came in after him.

"No fights in my store!" Mr. Lee yelled.

Dead Eye didn't listen. He just grinned. Skinny kid was cornered.

The supervillain was fixing to break him in half.

But it wasn't going down like that.

Because Dead Eye?

He made a BIG mistake.

That wasn't just any little kid hiding behind those bags of chips.

It was Marko Jackson.

When Marko gets scared, he gets mad.

And when Marko gets MAD . . .

THE CHANGE comes over him!

He turns into TOOTHPICK!

THE WORLD'S GREATEST SUPERHERO!

Fighter for justice! Defender of the weak!

And a couple feet taller than regular Marko.

He's still skinny. But it's a STRONG skinny. Arms and legs like steel wires!

And those skinny fingers of his?

They turn into FINGER SPEARS!

Razor sharp! Fast as lightning! Cut the bad guys up like shish kebab!

SQUICK! SMICK! ZICK!

Toothpick busted out of that snack aisle with his finger spears snicking!

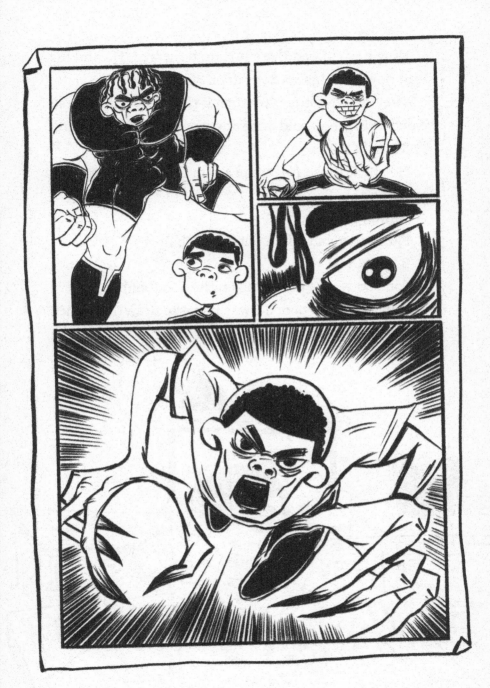

Now it was Dead Eye's turn to be scared. He and his Dead Boyz ran right out the door.

They didn't get far. Toothpick flew down the street, soared up in the air, and came down on them like a warbird!

SQUIIIICK!

He stuck those finger spears in deep, right between Dead Eye's—

BAM!

I jumped about a foot out of my chair.

BAM! BAM!

Somebody was pounding on the door behind me.

I set down the pencil I was using to draw Toothpick sticking it to Dead Eye.

BAM-BAM-BAM!

"Quit that pounding!" I yelled. Our apartment's so small, the front door's only about a foot from the kitchen table, where I was drawing. It sounded like J.R. was knocking on my skull.

"Let me in!"

I knew it was J.R. even before I heard his voice. At four o'clock on a Monday, he's the only other person in our building except old Mr. Hampton upstairs. And Mr. Hampton doesn't go around banging on people's doors.

I opened up for J.R. "Why you gotta pound so hard, man?"

"Why ain't you answering? You got headphones on or something?"

"Nah, I was just drawing." Sometimes when I'm making a comic, I get so into it, I stop living in the world. Dad says he could drop a bomb next to my chair, and I wouldn't notice.

J.R. squinted down at me. We're the same age, but he's about a head and a half taller than I am.

"You don't *look* like you got your butt whipped," he told me. "Did you make it home before Tyrell caught you?"

"Man, I don't know what you're talking about!"

That wasn't true. I knew what he was talking about. I just didn't want to talk about it.

But J.R. wouldn't let it go. "Dewayne said Tyrell and his crew chased you all the way from the bus stop to

5

the deli. Then Mr. Lee made them leave while he let you sneak out the back."

"Don't listen to Dewayne!" I told him. "He's just ignorant. None of that happened."

J.R. looked over my shoulder at the pages I was drawing. "You making a Toothpick about it?"

"Don't go looking at that! It's not done yet!"

Too late. J.R. pointed at my drawing of Dead Eye getting squicked. "Is that Tyrell?"

"No, man! That's a supervillain!"

"Looks like Tyrell. Got that same busted eye. You trying to pretend you kicked his butt?"

"Course not! Man, how many times I have to tell you? Toothpick is NOT ME!"

"Then how come he looks like you?"

"He doesn't! Do I wear a costume? Do I fly through the air? Do I have SPEARS ON MY FINGERS?"

"Bet you *wish* you did."

"Will you get out? Why are you even here?"

"Shoot some zombies, fam!" J.R. held up a copy of *Army of the Undead 3*.

My eyes bugged out. I'd been hearing about that game for months before it dropped.

"Let's fire it up," J.R. said. He was already halfway down the little hallway to the living room.

"I can't right now," I told him. "If my dad comes home and sees us, he'll take my GameBox away."

Dad's got a rule that I can't do any gaming on school days. Even if he didn't, part of me wanted to keep drawing. It takes a lot of work to make a good comic, and I was feeling it with this one. I felt like I should keep going while I was still in a groove.

But I'm not going to lie: part of me wanted to shoot zombies, too.

J.R. sat down on the couch. "Just a couple minutes!" he begged. "It's only four o'clock. Your dad ain't coming home for hours."

He had a point. Dad wouldn't be back from work until at least seven. I took one look at the comic I was drawing and another one at the TV. *Army of the Undead 3* was already booting up. It looked pretty dope.

I huffed out my breath and sat down on the couch next to J.R. "Okay," I told him. "But just for a little. We gotta quit at the first save point."

He handed me the second controller. "For sure! We'll just play a little."

"Twenty minutes."

"Half hour at the most."

CHAPTER 2

HOW IT ALL GOT STARTED

A pack of zombies was trying to eat me and J.R. in a shoe store when I heard the front door open. Dad was back from work.

First thing I thought was, *Why's he home so early?*

But when I checked the clock, it was seven-thirty. Which wasn't early at all.

Second thing I thought was, *Why's it so dark in here?*

Sun must've gone down, and we were too busy gaming to notice.

Third thing I thought was, *I better get off this couch before Dad kicks my butt.*

But it was too late. Dad came in, wearing his transit uniform and holding a bag of Chinese food.

"Aww, *heck* no, Marcus!"

"Just five more minutes! We're almost at a save point!"

"You at a QUIT point is where you're at." Dad flipped on the light and headed for the GameBox.

J.R. had been around enough to know what was coming. "Mr. Jenkins! Can I please have my game back before you take the box away?"

Dad ejected the game and flipped the disc to J.R. Then he unplugged the box and picked it up.

"Please don't take it, Dad!" I begged him. "We weren't even playing that long!"

He snorted out his nose. "Son, you were sitting in the dark! Like a vampire! And you got that glazed doughnut look."

He wasn't wrong. After three hours of blasting zombies, I *felt* like a glazed doughnut.

J.R. ducked past my dad and headed out the door. "Thanks for having me over, Mr. Jenkins!"

"Stay out of trouble, J.R."

"I will!"

Then he was gone, and it was just me and Dad and the Chinese food. And the GameBox he was about to go hide on the top shelf of his closet.

"Please don't take it away!" I begged him again.

Dad just shook his head. "Got a monkey on your back, son. Hate to see it. But you can't bargain with the devil. Just gotta walk away. Go cold turkey. Now get yourself cleaned up for dinner."

By the time I came back from the bathroom, Dad had picked up my comics from the kitchen table so he could lay out the chicken fried rice. He was staring at what I'd drawn.

"Somebody chase you home from school today?"

I grabbed the pages from him. "Dad! How many times have I told you? That's not me! Toothpick is made up! He's fictional!"

"I feel you. Just don't bring that one into school." He pointed at the last page, with the half-finished drawing of Toothpick stabbing Dead Eye with his finger spears. "I don't want to have to come in, talk to Ms. Kimble again about your anger issues."

"I DON'T HAVE ANGER ISSUES!"

"Then why are you yelling at me?"

It was a good question. Tell you the truth, I didn't know. I just yell sometimes.

I shrugged it off. "I dunno. Let's eat."

We stuffed our faces with fried rice for a while. Then all of a sudden, Dad went, "Oh! We gotta talk about something."

It's never good news when he says that.

"Whatever it is, I didn't do it," I told him.

He got up from the table. "Hang on. Let me get the laptop."

That definitely sounded bad. "Did one of my teachers email you? Already?" It was only the first full week of school. Seemed a little early to be getting in some email-your-dad kind of trouble.

"No, it was that after-school cat. The art teacher."

"Mr. Giles? Aw, man!" My school has this program called Afternoon Adventures, and Dad makes me go to it till six o'clock every day. It was starting tomorrow, and I'd told Dad to sign me up for the art class 'cause it was the only thing I liked.

But Mr. Giles teaches the art class. And last year, we had some beef. "What did he want?"

"He said you're real talented, and he likes you. But if you want to do after-school art, you gotta follow his rules."

"But it's so stupid! All I want to do is draw comics! And he's all into, like, making us do clay sculptures. And origami."

"What, like folding those little birds out of paper? That's dope."

"No, it isn't! It's the opposite of dope! It's UN-dope. It's dopeless!"

"I ain't gonna argue that, son. But if you don't want to make birds out of paper, you gotta sign yourself up for something besides art."

He had the laptop open by then, and he started looking on the Afternoon Adventures website for other stuff to sign me up for.

"I'm not playing basketball, Dad."

He got this sad look on his face, like he always does when I tell him I don't want to play basketball. But it's his fault for marrying my mom. She was about five feet tall, and when they got together to make me, her short genes kicked his tall genes in the butt.

"It's good practice, Marcus," he told me for like the fiftieth time. "You work on your skills now, and once you hit your growth spurt—"

"It's not happening, Dad! I'm like five growth spurts behind!"

"How about flag football?"

"No way."

"Soccer? Volleyball?"

"No sports, Dad."

"You gotta get your exercise!"

"I do! I ran all the way home today!"

"'Cause somebody chased you?"

"NO!"

"Don't get angry now."

"Don't make me angry!"

He went back to the list on the website.

"Just put me in study lab," I told him. "I can draw my comics and nobody'll bug me."

He clicked on study lab. Then he made a face.

"It's full up."

"Aw, man! Seriously?"

"How about martial arts?"

"I'm not signing up to get my butt kicked! I can get that for free just walking down the street."

"How about chess?"

"That's just a different way of getting my butt kicked."

"Musical theater?"

"Kill me now, Dad. Kill. Me. Now."

He scrolled through the list and blew out a big sigh. "You're making this hard, boy."

"Why do I even have to go to after-school? It's stupid!"

"Keeps you out of trouble. So you be productive! Make something of yourself." Then he lowered his voice. "Don't you want to make your mama proud?"

I lowered my voice, too. "Course I do," I told him.

What was I going to say? There was no arguing with that.

Dad looked at the list again. "How about filmmaking?"

"What's that?"

He squinted to read the fine print on the website. "'Make your own movies and online videos with the same tools and tricks the pros use! Learn to be a star in front of and behind the camera!' How's that sound?"

I shrugged. "Fine. Whatever. Sign me up for that."

And THAT . . . is how this whole movie thing got started.

CHAPTER 3

FIRST DAY OF FILM CLASS

Afternoon Adventures Filmmaking met in this empty English classroom with pictures of dead authors like Shakespeare and Toni Morrison all over the walls. (Being an author must be rough. Because whenever I see a picture of one? They're dead.)

Right away, I figured film class was going to stink. There were just four other kids in it, and the only one I knew was Khalid. He's in my grade. He's got these big thick glasses, and he's weird. But we're into the same comics, so we talk about them sometimes.

The other three kids were all a year older. There was a pretty girl with mad attitude. A quiet kid in a purple hoodie who deejayed the school dance last spring. And this tall, skinny girl I had words with once when she was laughing too loud on the bus.

I was hoping she didn't remember that. After I told her to pipe down, she dissed me hard in front of J.R. and

Dewayne. Then my stop came, and I had to get off the bus before I could think of a good clapback.

So I didn't even know her name. But I pretty much hated her guts already.

The class had two teachers, Darren and Trish. They seemed way too young and smiley to be regular teachers. Which was good, because the young smiley teachers will put up with a lot before they kick you out of class. And with that gangly mean girl from the bus around, I figured some stuff might go down.

I wasn't wrong about that.

Darren and Trish got things started by telling us all how they were in "film school," which I didn't even know was a kind of school. Then they asked us to say our names and why we were in the class.

Pretty Girl went first. Her name was Jazmin. She said, "I'm fixing to start my own channel on MeTube? Do makeup tutorials, maybe hair? Then I'll become an INFLUENCER. And brands will send me free swag! And THEN I can do unboxing videos where I open all the free swag on camera. And it'll just snowball from there."

Darren and Trish were all, "Yes, girl! You go AFTER that! We're going to help you take that channel to the NEXT level!"

"Well, I don't have the channel yet," said Jazmin. "It's just an idea."

"It's all good!" Trish told her. "You'll get there!"

"Gotta dream it before you can be it!" Darren clapped. "It's a journey! You're on the ROAD!"

Then it was Khalid's turn. He shrugged and kind of mumbled, "I like monster movies?"

Darren said, "Do you want to MAKE monster movies?"

"Because YOU CAN DO IT, Khalid!" Trish told him. "You can do ANYTHING you set your mind to!"

"Okay," said Khalid. "Maybe." Mostly, though, he just looked scared. I think Trish had too much energy for him.

The purple hoodie kid was Amari. He said he'd laid down some music tracks, and he wanted to create videos for them. "I just want to raise my edit game," he said.

"We can do that for you, brother!" Darren told him.

"Amen!" said Trish. "We're going to show you how to take those vids to the TOP of the charts! Make 'em go VIRAL!"

Darren and Trish were really working my nerves. I was starting to feel like I was in a TV commercial. And not a good one. A bad one.

Then they got to the nasty bus girl. And it went to a real strange place.

"Now it's our girl SIERRA'S turn!" Trish called out.

"Give it up for SIIIIEEEERRRAAAAA!" yelled Darren.

I was thinking, *I can't believe this. Nasty Bus Girl is the teachers' pet? ALREADY? Man, I should've just taken martial arts and got my butt kicked all day.*

She tried not to smile. But her face couldn't stop busting into this huge grin. She said, "My name's Sierra. And I just want to be . . . THE NEXT Taylor Berry."

"YESSSSS!" yelled Trish.

"You're gonna do it!" Darren told her. "YES, YOU ARE!"

I said, "Who's Taylor Berry?"

Everybody looked at me like I'd just said I didn't know who the president was.

"You don't know Taylor Berry?" said cute Jazmin, her eyes bugging out.

"He's a BOSS," Sierra told me. "He writes, directs, produces, and STARS in all his own movies."

Then I remembered who they were talking about. "Oh, THAT dude!" I said. "The one who dresses up like a nasty old lady?"

"That's him!" said Darren. "Brother, he is FUNNY."

I looked at that Sierra girl and said, "If y'all want to dress up like a nasty old lady, that's easy for you. 'Cause you most of the way there already."

She sat up about six inches taller in her chair. "You calling me nasty?"

"Not necessarily," I said. "I might just be calling you old."

"Now, let's not get hot," said Trish, turning all schoolmarmy.

"I'm DEFINITELY old compared to you," Sierra said. "'Cause you look like you about SIX."

"I'm old enough to whip your butt!" I shot back.

"Whoa, whoa, whoa!" Darren raised his hands like a referee. "Peace, brother!"

"What you gonna do, little leprechaun?" Sierra asked me. "Bite my knees?"

I'm not going to lie: that made me mad. I got so mad, I don't really remember what happened next. Except somebody knocked over a desk. And it might have been me.

It took a couple of minutes to get us all settled down and the furniture back in place.

After that, Trish gave us this speech that was all, "Peace and love, gotta get along, one big happy family, filmmaking's a team sport, blah blah blah blah blah."

And then finally, they were all, "Now tell us about YOU."

I said, "My name's Marcus. And I'm just here because study lab was full."

Darren said, "Do you want to MAKE MOVIES?"

I said, "NO, I DON'T. How about you just let me sit in that corner and draw my comics, and we'll all be good?"

And Trish said, "What KIIIIIND of comics do you draw?"

I said, "Superheroes."

Then Darren said, "Do you want to make a SUPERHERO MOVIE?"

And I gotta be honest: before he said it, I had not thought of that.

It's not like I'd never thought about a Toothpick movie.

In fact, that's pretty much ALL I ever think about. 'Cause I'm usually either drawing a comic or thinking about drawing a comic. And when I'm drawing a Toothpick story, it's like I'm watching a movie of it in my head. And I'm just trying to get the movie that's in my head down on the paper.

But I'd never thought that I could just straight-up MAKE A TOOTHPICK MOVIE.

I always figured, first I'd have to draw like a thousand Toothpick comics and make them a big hit as comic books. Then the movies would come a lot later. Like, around the same time as the Toothpick lunch boxes, and roller coasters, and underpants.

Because I want to make Toothpick HUGE! Bigger than big! Bigger than Superguy! Or Batguy! Or Spiderguy! Or any of those guys!

So I always knew SOMEDAY . . . there'd be Toothpick movies. A whole bunch of them.

But it wasn't until Darren asked me, sitting in that film class, that I got to thinking . . .

What if SOMEDAY . . . was TODAY?

And that just blew my mind.

All of a sudden, my thoughts were taking off like a rocket!

First, I was all, *What's the movie gonna be? Who's Toothpick gonna fight?*

The Doom? Purple Witch? Doctor Mindsuck?

Gotta be the Doom, man. He's the Death Master! King of All Evil!

Then I was like, *Wait—who's going to PLAY Toothpick? Like, as an actor?*

I looked around the room. Nobody seemed like they could even come close.

Then I realized: *IT'S ME, MAN!*

I could be Toothpick! I could be THE STAR of the whole thing!

Oh, man. Oh, man!

Oh man oh man OH MAN!

I could see it all in my head. I had a DREAM!

I don't know why I didn't have it earlier. But it didn't matter. 'Cause now I HAD it! And that dream was so big and tasty, I just about jumped out of my seat and ran around the room.

I was so excited, I had to sit on my hands to keep them from flying around while I started running through what the movie would be in my head.

Then I started running the movie ABOUT the movie—like, what would happen after it came out, and everybody loved it, and I was a star.

Then I went back to the movie. Then back to being a star. Then back to the movie again, and—

PLOP!

This twenty-page stack of paper fell out of the sky onto my desk.

I looked up at Trish. She was dropping stacks of paper in front of everybody. The pages all had holes punched in the side, and they were held together with these metal fasteners, like they were little books.

The top page was blank except for five words, in big letters:

PHONE ZOMBIES

By

Sierra Martinez

"What's this?" I asked Trish.

"The screenplay," she said.

"The what now?"

"The screenplay! The script! For the movie we're going to make!"

I looked around the room. Everybody was giving me the same kind of stares I got when I didn't know who Taylor Berry was.

"Where you been the last ten minutes?" Jazmin wanted to know.

"Marcus, have you heard a word we've been saying?" Darren asked.

"Course I have! But, uh . . . can you just run it by me again real quick?"

Darren held up one of the booklet things. "This is the SCREENPLAY," he said. "For the MOVIE. That we're all going to make TOGETHER."

"But I want to make a superhero movie!" I said.

"It's all good," said Darren. "And that can be your SIDE project. Just for you. But for our BIG project . . . that we all work on TOGETHER . . . and screen for everybody at the Fall Arts Showcase . . . we're going to make THIS script. That Sierra wrote."

I did NOT like the sound of that. I held up that girl's script like it was a rotten banana. "Where did this even come from?"

Nasty Sierra gave me a big sigh and rolled her eyes. "Like we SAID . . . if you were LISTENING . . . I wrote it during the summer film workshop!"

"Well, good for you!" I told her. "But that ain't fair! Why can't we make MY movie the big project?"

"Because duh! You don't have a screenplay!"

"YES, I DO!"

"Oh, please! You don't even know what a screenplay is!"

"I DO, TOO! I GOT ONE AT HOME!"

That was not exactly what you'd call a true statement. It was more like a lie.

But this girl didn't know that. And I had a whole mess of Toothpick comics in a box under my bed. So I figured I could use those to make a screenplay, or whatever you call it.

I mean, if this girl could make a screenplay, how hard could it be?

Darren had his hands up like a referee again. "Why don't we do this?" he said. "Marcus, you bring in your screenplay tomorrow. Let us read it. Then we'll ALL decide, TOGETHER, which one we want to use for the big project. Does that sound fair?"

"It sounds GOOD," I said. "But I don't know about fair. Because mine is SO AMAZING, it's gonna CRUSH hers."

I believed that. Because I had a dream now. And NOTHING was going to stop me.

Not even a what-do-you-call-it.

Screenplay.

That was going to be easy. And my movie was going to be DOPE.

CHAPTER 4

THE WORLD'S GREATEST SCREENPLAY!

"What you all excited about?" J.R. asked me. We were standing in the back of the city bus with Dewayne, coming home from Afternoon Adventures. They'd both been playing basketball, so they had that sweat stink on them.

"I ain't excited," I said.

"Then why you bouncing up and down like your butt's on fire?" Dewayne asked.

I decided not to tell them about the movie yet. It was way too early. I needed to make some progress on it first. At least get that screenplay done.

But then I just told them anyway.

"I'M MAKING A MOVIE!" I yelled.

"What kinda movie?"

"Superhero movie, man! Gonna be huge!"

Then I heard Nasty Sierra's snotty voice from way up near the front of the bus. "Is somebody being LOOOUUD back there?"

I didn't even turn around. But J.R. and Dewayne got up on their toes and looked past me at her.

"Yo, fam! Ain't that the girl threw shade on you that one time?"

Dewayne laughed. "Yeeeeeah! Made you look a fool!"

"Don't even start with her, man," I said. "She's just jealous. 'Cause she's in the film class, and we're fixin' to make MY movie instead of hers."

"This going to be a Toothpick movie?" J.R. asked me.

"Yeah, man! It's gonna be dope! Fight scenes! Special effects! All kinds of stuff."

"Who's gonna play Toothpick?"

"Me! I am!"

"You gonna have finger spears?"

"Course I am! I'm gonna fly, too! All of it! Just like in my comics!"

"How you gonna film yourself flying?"

That was actually a very good question.

"There's ways to do it," I told J.R.

I figured there must be. And Darren and Trish probably knew what they were. What else would they be learning in that film school?

"Can I be in your movie?" J.R. asked. "Can I play the bad guy?"

"Yeah, man! I'll hook you up. Make you a star, too!"

Dewayne shook his head and rolled his eyes. "Dawg, you ain't gonna make no movie."

"Yes, I am!"

"A superhero movie? Where you fly through the air and blow stuff up? Please."

"I'm doing it! And it's going to be DOPE!"

"Just like you was going to sell all your Toothpicks to Capital Comics?"

"I'm STILL going to do that!"

"Pfffft! You nothing but talk, Marcus."

That got me mad. Dewayne was a hater. Always had been.

But it was fuel for me. Just made me more determined to crush it!

I'd show Dewayne. I'd show EVERYBODY.

———

When we got back to our building, J.R. wanted to come upstairs and sneak the GameBox out of the closet where Dad hid it. But I wouldn't let him come in and shoot zombies, because I had to put my screenplay together. Soon as I got to the apartment, I went straight to my box of Toothpick comics.

I'd drawn a ton of them over the years. And I already knew which story I wanted to use for the movie. It was the first one I ever drew.

It was the most important, too. Because it had the first-ever battle with THE DOOM!

The Doom was Master of Evil. Death himself! In that first-ever comic, he tried to kill innocent people with the Ooze. It was this thick black death gunk. Got in people's bodies and made them sick.

Especially this one lady. Name was Angel. She was laid up in a hospital with the Ooze all in her. The Doom was fixin' to kill her dead. Take her soul away.

But Toothpick stopped the Doom cold! Messed him up good! Saved that Angel lady's life! She got all better, went back to her family. Toothpick was a hero.

My first version of that comic looked trash, because I was only nine when I made it. I barely knew how to draw yet.

But last summer, I went back and redrew it so I could send it to Capital Comics. When I did, I added an ORIGIN STORY. New version told all about how Toothpick got his powers from ancient African magic.

It was perfect for a screenplay. Plus, the summer school teacher let me make copies, so I had a couple extra.

The only problem was, the comic seemed kind of short for a whole movie. So I took the OTHER Toothpick comic I had copies of—which was about how he stopped the Doom from blowing up Center City with a bomb—and mashed them together.

Then I drew a dope-looking cover page. Like the one on Nasty Sierra's screenplay, only better:

TOOTHPICK FIGHTS THE DOOM!

BY

MARCUS JENKINS

I'd just finished up when Dad came home with burritos for dinner. While we ate them, I showed him my screenplay.

"Good job on that," he said. "Looks sharp."

"Gonna be amazing, Dad! Gonna be a whole movie! And I'm gonna play Toothpick! Everybody's gonna love it! I can't wait to turn this screenplay in!"

"That's a screenplay?" he asked.

"Yeah! It's the BOMB!"

"Huh." Dad rubbed his jaw like he was thinking it over. "You SURE that's a screenplay?"

"Course it is! Why wouldn't it be?"

"I just thought screenplays were like . . . words and not pictures. Like a play is."

"No, Dad! This is BETTER! It's got all the visuals! So you can see it in your head!"

He ate a bite of burrito. Then he nodded and gave me a big old smile. "Okay, then. Good on you, boy! Can't wait to see the movie."

"Me neither, Dad! It's going to be AMAZING!"

"I bet it will. Now quit bouncing up and down and eat that dinner."

I was so excited, I could hardly eat. Couldn't sleep that night, either.

And the whole next day at school, I couldn't sit still!

Because I knew the minute I walked in that film-making class? And dropped my screenplay on them? I was going to BLOW THEIR MINDS.

CHAPTER 5

EVERYBODY'S WRONG EXCEPT ME!

"WHAT DO YOU MEAN, IT'S NOT A SCREENPLAY?"

"Now, let's use our indoor voice," said Trish.

"THIS IS MY INDOOR VOICE!"

I was mad.

Way past mad.

Like I was fixin' to bust a vein in my head and explode.

"I feel you, brother," Darren told me. "I do! I know you're frustrated. But making a movie . . . it's like building a HOUSE. And to build that house, you need a BLUEPRINT. So all the plumbers and carpenters know the plan. That's what a screenplay is! It's like a blueprint for your movie. So all the people who work on it together—actors, directors, wardrobe people, what have you—they all know what's up."

"THIS can be a blueprint!" I yelled, shaking my Toothpick pages at him.

"Not really, though," Trish said. "And that's not a slam! Your comic is dope! I LOVE what you did with it!"

"Me too!" Darren chimed in. "You got mad skills! You're an ARTIST, brother!"

"But it's a COMIC," Trish told me. "And you can use a comic to MAKE a screenplay. But you need a screenplay to make a MOVIE. That comic is like having PICTURES of the house you want to build. When what you need is the BLUEPRINT."

"See, THIS is what a screenplay looks like." Darren picked up Nasty Sierra's stupid *Phone Zombies* script and turned the pages to show me the writing inside.

"But that one stinks!" I yelled. "My story's better!"

I was thinking, *How do they not see that? It's SO OBVIOUS!*

"How you know it's better?" Nasty Sierra asked. "Did you even read mine?"

"Yeah, I did!"

That wasn't true. And everybody knew it, so they all laughed. That just made me madder.

"Why don't you make it your SIDE project to turn that comic of yours into a screenplay?" Darren asked. But I wasn't having any of it.

"This is RIGGED!" I yelled. "It's a setup! You're all against me!"

"No, we're not, Marcus," Trish told me in her school-marmy voice. "We're just trying to build something TOGETHER."

"Making movies is a TEAM SPORT," Darren added.

"Well, I don't want to be on this team!" I told them. "It's not fair! It's like—it's like—"

I tried to think of the world's worst team. But I don't watch enough sports. So I had to come up with a different example.

"This is like NORTH KOREA, man! It's a DICTATOR-SHIP! We ain't got no rights in here! We all gotta bow down and get blown up by nuclear weapons!"

They all laughed. Then Nasty Sierra said, "Daaaang! Somebody been listening in social studies." Then they all laughed some more.

"You are FUNNY, brother," Darren told me.

That set me off. If there's one thing that gets me hot, it's people laughing at me.

"I'M SERIOUS!" I yelled. "This ain't no democracy! Y'all are BRAINWASHED!"

"You want a democracy?" Sierra asked. She looked around the room. "Raise your hand if you want to make Marcus's comic book the group project."

My hand shot up to the ceiling. But I was the only one.

"Now raise your hand if you want to make *Phone Zombies*," she said.

Everybody raised their hands: Jazmin, Amari, Khalid... even Darren and Trish.

I could feel my face burning up. They were all against me. Every one of them.

"You can still do your comic book movie on the side," Trish said in a calm-yourself-down voice.

But I was way past that.

There was only one thing to do.

"I'M OUTTA HERE!" I screamed. "I QUIT!"

Then I got up and walked out that door forever.

CHAPTER 6

I'M A LONE WOLF, MAN!

Here's a thing you should probably know about me: I do not always think things through.

It's like, sometimes my mouth will start running. And it'll get, like, a mile away before my brain puts its shoes on.

That's pretty much what happened when I quit the filmmaking class. Because storming out of that room was EASY.

But figuring out where to go after I'd stormed out was HARD.

There were Afternoon Adventures classes in pretty much every room of the school. But I wasn't signed up for any of them except filmmaking, so I couldn't go into them.

I couldn't just walk out the door and go home, either. Because the only door in the building that doesn't have an alarm on it is the front door.

And Officer Shirley was sitting right there at her desk in the entranceway. She won't let you leave Afternoon Adventures before six, unless you either got a note from your dad or you can run faster than her.

Now, I can definitely run faster than Officer Shirley. But that just makes the problem worse. Because she knows who I am. And she'll still be there tomorrow. So if I run away from her, emails will get sent, my dad will get called, and it'll just be an all-around pain in the butt.

I know this, because it happened last year after I ran out of art class over that whole origami bird situation.

So what I wound up doing this time was sort of pacing up and down the hallways until Ms. Dorothy, who runs the whole program, found me and wanted to know why I wasn't in class.

Then she tried to make me go BACK to the film class. But I wasn't having that.

So then she made me sit in a chair next to Officer Shirley until six o'clock.

That wasn't the worst part, though.

The worst part was that J.R. and Dewayne were the first kids out, and they saw me sitting with Officer Shirley.

So the whole way home on the bus, they were on my case about it.

"You get kicked out of class already?"

"No, man! I quit! Those teachers are fools. They don't know nothing."

Dewayne snorted. "I knew you weren't going to make that movie."

"What you mean? I'm STILL making the movie!"

"All by yourself?"

"Yeah! Course I am!"

"Man, you can't make a movie by yourself!"

"I can, too! You know Taylor Berry? Dude does it ALL himself. Acts. Directs. The other stuff."

"What's the other stuff?"

"It's filmmaking stuff. You wouldn't understand."

True fact: I didn't understand, either. I'd quit the class before we got around to learning anything about how to make a movie. But I wasn't going to tell J.R. and Dewayne that. And I figured once I got home, I could look it up on the internet.

"So let me get this straight," Dewayne said in a snotty voice. "Yesterday, you was gonna be a superhero movie actor? And today, you gonna be Taylor Berry?"

"Bet!"

J.R. looked confused. "You gonna dress up like an old lady?"

"No, man! I'm gonna be Toothpick! I'm just a FILM-MAKER like Taylor Berry."

Dewayne was shaking his head. "Dawg, please! You ain't gonna make no movie."

"Bet!"

"Okay. Twenty dollars!"

Before I knew it, I was shaking hands on a twenty-dollar bet with Dewayne.

That gave me a scared feeling in my stomach. Because

I did NOT have twenty dollars. And I did NOT know how to make a movie.

Then J.R. and Dewayne started talking basketball. So I took my phone out and did a search for "how to make a movie."

But my phone's about a hundred years old, the battery's trash, and Dad won't pay for a data plan. So I was still just trying to find some open Wi-Fi when it ran out of charge and died.

When we got home, J.R. tried to talk his way into my apartment.

"C'mon! Let's just take the GameBox out for a minute! Get to the next save point! Then we'll put it back in the closet before your dad comes home."

"No, man! I got work to do!"

"What kind of work?"

I showed him my *Toothpick Fights the Doom!* comic. "I gotta turn this into a screenplay! That's like the blueprint for a movie."

"Can I still be in it? Can I play the Doom?"

"Not if you don't leave me alone and let me get to work!"

After I got rid of J.R., I took out the laptop and searched up "how to make a movie."

It turned out there are a LOT of sites on the internet that can tell you how to make a movie.

And every single one of them was TERRIFYING.

Because it was SO MUCH WORK!

And I didn't understand ANY of it!

I didn't even know half the words!

Preproduction? Storyboarding? Cinematography?

Cinema-WHAT?!

That scared feeling I got in my stomach when I made the bet with Dewayne took over my whole body. I felt like I was having a heart attack.

It got so bad, I had to lie down and curl up in a little ball on the floor.

I was still lying there when Dad came home with burgers.

"What's the matter, son? Got a bellyache?"

"I got a BRAIN ache, Dad."

"Get yourself off that floor. Let's talk it out."

While we ate the burgers, I told him everything.

"So what you going to do?" he asked when I was done.

"I dunno," I said. "Can I borrow twenty dollars to pay Dewayne?"

He shook his head. "Forget about that fool. What you going to do about the movie?"

"What you mean?"

"Still going to make it, aren't you?"

"Dad! I can't make a movie all by myself! It's too hard!"

"So get back to that class."

"I can't."

"Why not?"

I tried to imagine it. But all I could see were the looks on Nasty Sierra's and everybody's faces when they'd laughed at me.

"I just can't," I told Dad. "There's no way."

"So you just going to up and quit? What would your mama say about that?"

Hearing him mention Mom got me mad and sad at the same time.

"She ain't here! She don't have to sit in class with those people, gettin' laughed at!"

"Seems to me—"

"NO, DAD! I just can't!"

It was the truth.

It hurt like heck to give up my movie dream. I'd only had it for a day. But it was SO DOPE!

I was going to make Toothpick come to life!

I was gonna fly through the air! Beat down the Doom! Save that Angel's life!

And I was going to be a MOVIE STAR!

Except now I wasn't. Because there was no way I was going back and letting Nasty Sierra and the rest of them laugh at me again.

Dad huffed out a big sigh. Then he shoulder-shrugged. "It's your call, son. Just hope you like singing and dancing."

"Why's that?"

"Because I got an email from the Afternoon Adventures lady. She said if you want to drop out of filmmaking, everything else is full up now except musical theater."

CHAPTER 7

RETHINKING THAT WHOLE LONE WOLF BUSINESS

Me and the musical theater class just wasn't a good fit for anybody. Half an hour into it, the teacher already had me in a time-out at the back of the auditorium.

Sitting alone in the back was actually a big improvement over being onstage, trying to sing and dance. I was thinking up ways I could get myself into a time-out every day when Nasty Sierra walked in.

She looked around and saw me sitting there. Then she came over and sat right by me.

"How's this going for you?" she asked.

"It's all good."

"Yeah? You like this class better than filmmaking?"

"Sure do. 'Cause YOU ain't in it."

She straightened up, like she was going to clap back. But then she leaned in toward me and took the sass out of her voice. "Look, dude, I'm sorry we got off wrong. Some of that's on me. I apologize. And I came here to ask you . . . to please come back to filmmaking."

I just stared at her. This girl HAD to be playing me. But she looked serious.

"Darren and Trish make you come over here?"

She shook her head. "We talked about it. But it was my idea."

That didn't make any sense. This girl hated me! And I hated her!

"Why you want me to come back?"

"You want the truth?" she asked.

"No, I want a pack of lies! Duh."

"Okay, real talk." She took a deep breath. "I want you to act in my movie."

Now she was making even LESS sense.

"Heck no! I don't care about your dumb movie!"

"I know that! But you care about YOUR movie. Don't you?"

"Maybe."

I'd spent the whole last day trying to forget I ever had the idea to make a Toothpick movie. But it was tough letting that dream go. I still wanted it bad. I just didn't see how I could get it.

"I'll make you a deal," Sierra told me. "You act in my movie, and I'll help you make yours. Scripting, shooting, editing, all of it."

I didn't know what half that stuff was. But it sounded like what was on all those lists I saw on the internet. Ones that made me curl up in a ball on the floor.

All of a sudden, I got to thinking: *What if my movie dream ISN'T dead?*

The thought of it made me want to bust out of my seat.

But this girl HAD to be playing me.

"Man, you just trying to wind me up!"

"I'm not! I'm serious. Darren and Trish will help you, too. But if they can't do something, I promise I got you."

"Why would you help me?"

"So you'll help ME. I want you to act in my movie."

"Why you want me in it?"

"Because it's a comedy. And you're FUNNY."

So that was it. This girl wanted to goof on me.

"Well, you're funny-LOOKING!" I told her. "Gangly giraffe-neck girl—"

"I'm not throwing shade! Being funny's a GOOD thing!"

"No, it ain't! I don't want people laughing at me!"

She rolled her eyes. "You don't get it. They won't be laughing AT you. They'll be laughing WITH you. Ain't nobody ever told you how funny you are? Especially when you get mad! The way you huff and puff? You're like Tevin Bart!"

Tevin Bart was a movie star. And he was for-real funny.

But he was something else, too.

"You're just saying that 'cause I'm SHORT!"

"Oh, man! No, I'm not! If short was all you were, I wouldn't be here! But you short AND funny! Why don't you own it? It could be like your superpower!"

I thought about all this for a minute. It was pretty wild.

"So what you're saying is . . . you want ME . . . to star in your movie—"

"I didn't say STAR in it. I said ACT in it. You'd be the sidekick. Not the main character. But you'll still get a lot of good lines."

"Who's the main character?"

"That's me." She wrinkled her nose in a grin. "You ain't the only one around here with a superpower."

"So all I got to do is act in your movie? That's it? Nothing else?"

"Of course! You don't know how to DO nothing else!"

"I can draw!"

"And that's REAL helpful when you're making a MOVIE." She rolled her eyes. "Look, you MIGHT not even be able to act. But I'll take a chance on that. 'Cause when you get mad? You look HILARIOUS. The way those eyes bug out is EXACTLY like Tevin Bart."

I had to admit, I was starting to like the sound of this. Tevin Bart might be short. But he was also a very handsome individual. Plus, he was famous. Probably rich, too.

But the important thing was my Toothpick movie.

"So if I do this for you," I asked Sierra, "you going to make my movie for me?"

"Oh, heck, no!"

"See, there it is—"

"I'm going to HELP you make your movie. Along with Darren and Trish and the other kids. It's YOUR movie—you still gotta put the work in. But we can help. YOU help us, and WE help you. What do you say?"

"I gotta think about it," I told her.

Then I thought about it. For like two seconds.

"Okay," I said. "It's a deal."

Way down on the stage at the other end of the room, the teacher was running all the musical theater kids through some kind of dance step. I jumped up, threw my arms in the air, and screamed at them: "I'M OUTTA HERE! I QUIT!"

True fact: that theater teacher looked even happier than I was. I'd just saved her a whole lot of time-outs.

And I had a dream again!

I was MAKING A MOVIE!

Just as soon as somebody showed me how to do it.

CHAPTER 8

I WRITE A SCREENPLAY! (FOR REAL THIS TIME)

After I came back to film class, Darren sat me down. Gave me another lecture about how making movies is a team sport, we all gotta have each other's backs, blah blah blah. I promised him I was good with it.

Then he showed me how to write a screenplay. Turns out, there's a lot of rules.

Most of them are boring.

Like, the first line of every scene has to start with "INT." or "EXT." Those are short for "Interior" and "Exterior." You put those in so people know if your scene's inside or outside.

Next, you write where the scene happens. Like "KITCHEN" or "CLASSROOM" or "GIANT TANK FULL OF SHARKS."

Then you have to end that first line with the time of day. Like "DAY" or "NIGHT" or . . .

Zzzzzzzzgggghhhh.

Sorry. Fell asleep for a minute. Because that's how boring these rules are.

After he told me all the rules, Darren showed me how to download a screenwriting program so I could type my script on Dad's laptop. When I came home that night, I got it all set up and started writing *Toothpick Fights the Doom!*

The first two lines were easy:

EXT. SKY ABOVE CENTER CITY - DAY
TOOTHPICK's flying through the air.

Then I got stuck. Didn't know what to write next.

Should he fight the Doom now? Or is it too soon? Should he talk to somebody first? Who's he going to talk to? He's way up in the air!

I figured I should start with Toothpick down on the ground instead.

So I deleted those first two lines. Then I started over:

EXT. SIDEWALK - CENTER CITY - DAY
TOOTHPICK's walking down the street.

Then I got stuck again.

What street is he on? Where's he going? Who else is there? They going to talk? What do they talk about?

Then I got hungry. So I ate some leftovers.

Then I went back to the script.

Still couldn't figure out what to write next.

So I took a little break. Went online, watched some MeTube videos. Read up on all the comic books that were coming out soon.

Then I got to feeling bad about not working on my script. So I went back to it.

Got stuck again. Right away.

I got so stuck, I decided to do my homework.

This was NOT normal.

I don't DO my homework. Except that night, I did. Because it was easier than trying to write that screenplay.

Dad came home about ten. He'd been working late. So had I.

"Why ain't you in bed, boy?"

"I'm writing a screenplay!"

I'd written about five more lines by then. Trouble was, I'd thrown out four of them.

Dad looked around. "Did you clean up the apartment?"

"A little bit. Writing is HARD, Dad!"

Next day in film class, I asked Darren for help again.

"I didn't know what to write!" I told him. "I kept getting stuck!"

He nodded. "I feel you. Here's how you fix that: with an OUTLINE."

"Outline?"

"Yeah! It's like making a road map. So you know where you're going. Write down all the stuff you want to put in the story. Scenes. Characters. Beginning. Middle. End. Put it all in your outline. Now you got a map! So when you sit down to write, you won't get stuck. You just follow your map!"

"That's all I gotta do?"

Darren gave me a big old smile. "That's it, brother! Write the outline. Then write the script. It'll be AMAZING!"

"You think so?"

"I KNOW IT! Keep it up, Marcus! You're on the right track!"

Then Darren went off to help Amari with some music video stuff. Nasty Sierra was typing on a school laptop a couple of desks from me. She must've been listening in. Because she leaned toward me and said, "You want to know the truth?"

"About what?"

"What Darren said."

"He didn't tell me the truth?"

"He told you HALF the truth. Making an outline's a good idea. You should do that."

"So what part was a lie?"

"The part where he said your script's gonna be amazing."

That set me off. "MIND YOUR OWN BUSINESS, gangly giraffe-neck girl!"

Everybody looked over at us, thinking there was going to be a fight. But Nasty Sierra didn't clap back. She just rolled her eyes. "You ever write a screenplay before?"

"You know I haven't!"

"That's why it won't be amazing yet. First time you drew a comic, was it good?"

I thought back to my first-ever Toothpick. "No. It was trash."

"Right. Then you did it again. And you got BETTER. Same with writing. You gotta sit your butt in the chair. Write the BAD version first. Then you REwrite it. Make it GOOD. But you can't write the good version till AFTER you write the bad version."

"That sounds like a lot of work," I said.

"Heck yeah, it is!" She pointed at the laptop in front

of her. "Know what I'm doing now? I'm rewriting *Phone Zombies*."

"Ain't that script done? Said you spent all summer on it!"

"I did! And it's good. But now I know YOU'RE playing the sidekick. And you are ALL kinds of different from who I had in my head for that part. So now I gotta go back and rewrite the scenes with your character in them."

"So you just gonna keep rewriting it forever?"

"No. Eventually, we'll shoot it. But until then? Long as I can make it better, I'll keep at it."

I thought about this for a bit.

"Say I write this script. Then how do I REwrite it? Like, how do I know WHAT I gotta rewrite to make it better?"

"You get somebody to READ it," she told me. "Then they can tell you what needs fixing. But it's gotta be somebody who knows what's up. Can't just give it to your friends or parents. 'Cause they want to be supportive. But they don't know from screenplays! So they'll just tell you it's great, instead of telling you the truth."

"Darren and Trish gonna tell me the truth?"

Sierra scrunched up her nose. "Maybe a little. But they mostly just cheerleaders. Rather make you feel good than make your script better. I'D tell you the truth, though."

"Bet you would. You'd love dunking on me."

She wrote her email address on a piece of paper. "Here. After you write the script, send it to me. I'll give you the real."

I spent the whole rest of film class making an outline. Wrote down everything I wanted to happen in *Toothpick Fights the Doom!*

When I got home that night, I looked at all my old Doom-fighting comics to get inspired. Then I went back to writing the screenplay. It was still hard. But it was a lot easier with an outline. I got about three pages done before I went to bed. Enough for Toothpick to find out the Doom was killing people with the Death Ooze.

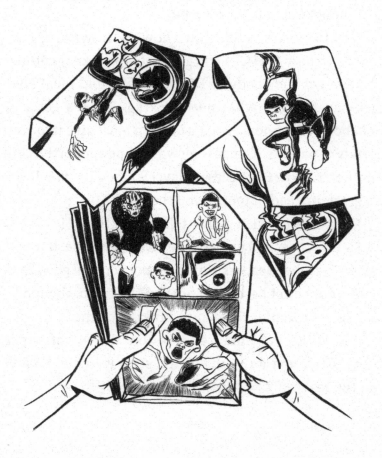

Next day was Saturday. I got up early.

And what I WANTED to do was watch TV. But what I DID . . . was keep writing.

Round ten o'clock, J.R. knocked on my door, wanting to shoot zombies. But I made him go away.

By lunchtime, I had six more pages. The Doom tried to kill that Angel lady in the hospital. Then Toothpick busted him!

They had a big old fight. Toothpick messed the Doom up good! Saved the lady's life!

I got so excited writing the fight scene, I had to get up and run back and forth down our hallway a few times.

Then I went back at it. Wrote up the whole part about the Doom with the nuclear bomb.

At 3:32 p.m., I finished! The whole thing! Twelve pages!

Last two lines were straight out of Darren's rules:

FADE OUT.

THE END

I'd done it! I wrote a whole screenplay!

It felt SO GOOD!

I emailed it to Sierra. Then I called up J.R. Spent the rest of the day shooting zombies.

That felt good, too! 'Cause I deserved to kick back after all that work.

CHAPTER 9

SIERRA READS
MY SCREENPLAY

Writing a screenplay is hard.

Know what else is hard? Waiting for somebody to READ your screenplay and tell you if it stinks.

When I finished writing it, I thought it was great! I was a genius!

But half an hour later, I was thinking it stunk. And I was just a fool.

Ten minutes after that, I thought it was great again.

I just didn't know. I needed that feedback! But Sierra was taking her sweet time with the email.

"Why you keep looking at your phone?" J.R. asked me. We were on my couch, playing *Army of the Undead 3*. I had my phone plugged in so the battery wouldn't die. Kept checking it for a reply every time we hit a save point.

"Waiting for an email."

"From who?"

"None of your business."

Then I thought of something. "You want to read my script? For the movie?"

J.R. got this look like I'd asked him to pick a booger out of my nose. "Do I have to?"

"You going to play the Doom, ain't you?"

"Heck yeah!"

"Then you gotta read the script!"

"I'll read it later."

I bugged J.R. for about four hours straight. Finally, he agreed to take a look. I showed him the script on Dad's laptop.

He stared at it for a while.

"'EXT.' What's that mean?"

"Short for exterior. Means it's outside. Man, don't stop at the first word! Keep going!"

He gave it maybe ten more seconds. Scrolled up and down a little. Then he handed back the laptop.

"It's good."

"You didn't read it!"

"I read enough! It's good."

"Man, that is weak!"

"I'll read more later."

He didn't read more later.

By the middle of Sunday morning, I was fixin' to pull my hair out.

"Why you so wound up?" Dad asked me.

"Waiting for this girl to read my script. She won't email me back."

"Want me to read it before I go to work?" Dad's got a second job he goes to on Sundays.

"Maybe?" Soon as I said that, I got a bad feeling in my stomach. Like I wanted to barf. "Second thought, no. Don't read it."

"You sure?"

"Yeah. You'll just tell me it's good even if it's trash."

"That's true. I would."

Right after Dad left for work, I got an email from Sierra:

I read the script and made notes. Text me before 10:30 and I'll drop it off on my way to church.

BAM! That barfy feeling hit my stomach again. I texted the number she gave me:

> Its Marcus. Just email the notes

> I can't. Hand-wrote them on script

> Cant u type them up

No it's a lot

When I saw that, my barfy feeling got ten times worse.

We can just talk tomorrow

if u want

No come by now

There was no way I was gonna let that barfy feeling just sit there for a whole day. I texted her my address. She said she'd drop by ASAP.

Our door buzzer's busted, so I went down to wait on the front stoop in case she was early.

Within ten minutes, I'd checked my phone so much, my battery was down to one percent. I texted Sierra:

WHERE R U

I was staring at that dot-dot-dot, waiting on her answer, when my battery died.

NO! NOOO!

I couldn't go back upstairs and plug it in. What if she came by and I missed her?

Just had to wait on the stoop.

So that's what I did.

For HOURS. And they felt like YEARS.

I kept looking up and down the street for her.

Why wasn't she showing? It was making my brains melt!

I couldn't believe she was blowing me off like that!

Felt like I'd been on that stoop half my life when J.R. came outside.

"Why you running up and down the steps?"

"I'm not! Just sitting here."

"Why you sitting here?"

"None of your business."

"Want to play some GameBox?"

"Not right now."

"Why not?"

"Just don't."

"C'mon, fam. You just sitting out here, bouncing up and down."

"Leave me alone! Got stuff to do!"

"What stuff?"

"None of your business!"

"Don't be all secretive."

"Don't be all nosy!"

Just then, I saw Sierra turn the corner at the end of the block. She had a backpack on her shoulder, and she was wearing a dress. My stomach started going flippy again.

"Get inside!" I told J.R. "I'll buzz you in a little."

"Buzzer don't work."

"I'll knock on your door! Just get out of here!"

"How long you gonna be?"

"I don't know!"

"Can I play your GameBox?"

"No!"

"Your dad won't mind! It's the weekend! C'mon. Let me borrow your keys."

"Then I'm locked out!"

"I'll throw them down to you. Out the window. C'mon. Hook me up."

Sierra was only two houses away. I had to get rid of J.R. in a hurry.

I threw my keys at him. "GET OUT OF HERE!"

He took my keys and went inside just in time. A second later, Sierra was in front of my stoop. That dress she was wearing looked all kinds of strange on her. She wasn't usually the dress-wearing type.

"What's up?" she asked, all casual. Like she hadn't just rolled up sixty hours late.

"WHERE YOU BEEN?" My stomach was extra-flippy.

"Told you I was running behind—so I'd come by after church instead of before. Didn't you get my text?"

"Naw, my phone died."

She screwed up her face. "You're at HOME. Why didn't you recharge it?"

"Just would've died again. I got like three minutes of battery."

"Literally? You charge your phone, full up—and it dies in THREE MINUTES?"

I shrugged. "I can get five or six if I keep it in low power mode."

Her eyes got big. "Oh, man. I gotta use that in *Phone Zombies!*"

She took off her backpack and unzipped the pocket. My stomach triple-flipped 'cause I thought she was getting my script out.

But then she took out a pen and a little notebook. Started writing in it.

"What you doing?"

"Writing this down so I don't forget."

"WHAT ABOUT MY SCREENPLAY?"

"Chill! I got you."

She put away the notebook. Then she pulled out some printed pages. Held them close so I couldn't see what was on them.

"That my screenplay? What you think of it?" I was halfway to barfing, and my head was starting to get dizzy.

She got a weird look on her face, like she was chewing some food and thought it might be off. "It could be good."

"COULD be?"

"Yeah. Just needs work."

"What kind of work?"

"Like . . . a LOT of work. Here's my notes." She handed me the script.

When I saw the first page, my jaw pretty much hit the sidewalk from the top step.

She'd written her notes in red pen. And there was so much red on that page, it looked like somebody bled to death on it.

I started turning pages. Red ink everywhere.

This wasn't just murder. It was MASS murder.

"I know it seems like a lot—"

"SEEMS like? You want me to rewrite every dumb word?"

She shrugged, like *maaaybe*. "Remember how I said you gotta write the bad version before you can write the good one?"

"So it's BAD?" I was starting to lose it.

"Not bad-bad. But it's not a story yet. It's just a bunch of stuff that happens."

"That's what a story is!"

"No, a story is a bunch of stuff that happens FOR A REASON. This don't have the reasons yet. There's no WHY. Or BECAUSE. Like, you got Toothpick just kind of wandering around for a couple pages—then all of a sudden, we're in this old lady's hospital room—"

"SHE'S NOT OLD!" I yelled. "She's thirty-one!"

Sierra looked confused for a second. "Okay, that is real specific. But who IS she? Why does the Doom attack HER and not somebody else? Gotta be a REASON."

"Sometimes there ain't no reason!" I said. "Sometimes bad stuff just happens to people!"

I got a lump in my throat when I said that. Had to swallow hard to get rid of it.

"Yeah, in LIFE, stuff just happens," Sierra said. "But in MOVIES, there's always a reason. Like, why's Toothpick even a superhero? How'd he get his powers?"

"ANCIENT AFRICAN MAGIC!" I yelled.

"But HOW?" she yelled back. "Did he go to Africa? Did Africa come to him? And ain't that corny? It's the same way Black Leopard got HIS powers."

"So what? Black Leopard's dope!" Next to Spiderguy, Black Leopard was my favorite superhero.

"But don't you want to come up with something of your own? So you ain't just ripping him off?"

"I AIN'T RIPPING OFF BLACK LEOPARD! His powers come from Blakanda! Toothpick ain't never been to Blakanda!"

Sierra got a nasty smirk on her face. "So where he get his powers from? EAST Blakanda? Blakanda Heights?"

I got so mad, I would've swung at her if she weren't a girl. And also about two feet taller than me.

"Man, ain't no Blakanda Heights in my story!"

"Ain't NOTHING in your story that tells us why!"

"Why's there gotta be a why?"

"So we CARE. So it MATTERS to us. You ain't gotta spell everything out in the script. But you gotta know it for yourself. Then give the audience just enough to hook them in. You gotta know: What's the Doom want? What's Toothpick want? What's so important about this lady in the hospital that they gotta fight over her? And why does . . . ?"

Sierra kept asking questions. But I quit listening. I couldn't figure out why she was throwing so much shade on my script.

Then it hit me.

"So, like, what if the Doom and Toothpick come from the same—"

"I SEE WHAT'S UP!" I yelled at her. "You tryin' to run out the clock! Make me rewrite my script till the class is done and there ain't no more time to make my movie! So you don't have to help me with it!"

Her eyes got all big and surprised. "THAT'S what you think?"

"Yeah! It's obvious!" I knew I'd busted her.

She laughed it off. "Fine! Don't rewrite it. Don't change a word." She slung her backpack over her shoulders. "We'll break down the scenes tomorrow and start casting it. Shoot it all next weekend. Thank you, next."

She started to walk away.

"Wait!"

"What?"

"You serious? We can shoot it next weekend?" I opened up the script to one of those bloody-note pages and showed it to her. "I don't have to do all this work?"

"You don't HAVE to do nothing, Marcus," she told me. "It's YOUR movie. I'm just trying to help you."

My face split in a big old grin. She'd been pulling my chain the whole time with those sorry notes.

"So you gonna help me shoot it? Like you promised?"

Sierra grinned right back. "For certain! I just gave you them notes 'cause I thought you wanted to make a GOOD movie."

She started walking again.

"WAIT!" I was getting confused. "So if we shoot it like this, just how I wrote it—it won't be good?"

"Oh, Lord, no! It'll be AWFUL. But I ain't fussed about that. It's YOUR movie. See you tomorrow."

I watched her go till she turned the corner out of sight.

I wasn't grinning anymore. Instead, I was . . .

I didn't even know what. Mad? Sad? Confused? Tired? All of them at once?

I flipped through the script. Just about all the white space was full up with that red ink. Sierra must've written about a hundred notes. Big questions. Little questions. Questions I didn't even understand—

"OWWW!" Something hit me on the head.

It was my house keys. I looked up. J.R. was sticking his head out my living room window.

"You want to play some GameBox?"

I took a deep breath, then blew it all out in a hard sigh.

"No, man. I got work to do."

CHAPTER 10

I REWRITE MY SCREENPLAY (UGH!)

Fact: when you rewrite a script, it ain't the writing that's hard.

It's figuring out WHAT to write that kills you.

I had to think up answers to a million questions.

Some of it was stuff I'd never thought about. Like, *Why's the Doom so evil?*

Other stuff, I THOUGHT I knew already. Like how Toothpick got his name and his powers. And what makes him change from a normal kid to a superhero.

But once Sierra called all that stuff out, my old ideas didn't seem dope enough anymore. They didn't fit together. And they were mostly just me ripping off other superheroes.

We talked it out a couple of times on the bus to school.

"Why you name him Toothpick?" Sierra asked me. "Does it mean anything?"

"Just means he's skinny."

"So why not call him Beanpole? Or Scrawny? Or Giraffe Neck?"

"I dunno. Toothpick's what his grammy called him."

"Toothpick got a grammy?"

"Can't superheroes have grammies?"

"Guess so. But is she in the movie? You gonna have a Supergrammy?"

"Naw! That's corny."

"She give him his powers, too? Grammy got that ancient African magic?"

I didn't just have to change where Toothpick got his powers from. I had to change the way his powers come out when he gets mad, too. That was just me straight-up stealing from the Impossible Bulk.

And his finger spears were basically SuperWolf's claws. But I kept those, because they looked way too dope to get rid of.

The other stuff had to go, though. It just wasn't good enough. I wanted my movie to be GREAT! And I knew Sierra was right. It wasn't there yet.

Trouble was, I didn't know what to change all that stuff TO.

I spent WEEKS trying to think it through. Lying in bed, sitting in class, walking down the street, standing in the shower, staring at my homework. Every other minute, my brain was chewing on it.

And I couldn't come up with ANYTHING good!

I'd get little bits and pieces of ideas. Like, Khalid and I got to talking in film class once. I was running ideas by him for how Toothpick got his name. And Khalid said, "What if they call him Toothpick 'cause he keeps a toothpick in his mouth? Like tough guys do?"

That didn't seem right. But it got me thinking maybe I SHOULD have some kind of actual toothpick in the story. Like as a weapon or something.

Next day, I was out for a walk, 'cause Trish told me people think better sometimes when they go for a walk. I passed this tree on the street with a branch all splintered up from getting hit by the roof of a truck going by.

That gave me an idea: What if it just LOOKED like a toothpick? But it was really a SPLINTER?

From something bigger? That had magic powers?

Like a . . . Staff of Power?

And the toothpick was a little sliver of it? But it had the power in it, too?

BAM! That was SOLID! I was thinking, *I should go on walks more often.*

Then I turned a corner and ran into big busted-eye bully Tyrell and his crew coming the other way.

My walk turned into a run REAL fast.

Soon as I got home, I wrote that Staff of Power idea down so I wouldn't forget it.

Then I started thinking about where that sliver of staff might have come from.

Like, what if it was part of some age-old battle between good and evil?

For control of the UNIVERSE?

That seemed cool. But I didn't know how Toothpick figured into it. He was just a normal kid before he got his superpower.

I chewed on that for a couple of days.

Then one morning, J.R. and I showed up at the bus stop before school. This grimy dude was lying on the bench. Sound of us coming must've woken him up. Because when we got close, he shot up real fast.

Then he looked around, all confused. Like he didn't know how he got there.

Like he just woke up on the wrong planet.

"OH, MAN!" I yelled.

J.R. stared at me. Grimy dude did, too.

"What is it?" J.R. asked.

"Nothing," I said.

But it wasn't nothing. It was a BRAINSTORM! My whole Toothpick origin story fell into place like a lightning bolt!

A couple of stops later, Sierra got on the bus. I was flying.

"I figured it out!" I told her. "The Doom's Master of Evil! Right? But not on Earth. Outer space! Another dimension! Astral Plane or some such. And he got an archenemy—the Master of GOOD! Who's like . . . a prince or something. Rules the universe with a Staff of Power! But the Doom and his evil army try to take him down! They go at it! Giant battle! Prince with his Staff of Power, Doom with his Black Death Ooze—"

"Ohh-kaaay . . ."

"Then, KA-BLOOM! The Doom blows up the prince's Staff of Power! It's busted in a million pieces! Evil's going to conquer the universe! That prince dude's fixin' to die! EXCEPT . . . he's got this ONE TINY LITTLE SLIVER of that Staff of Power left."

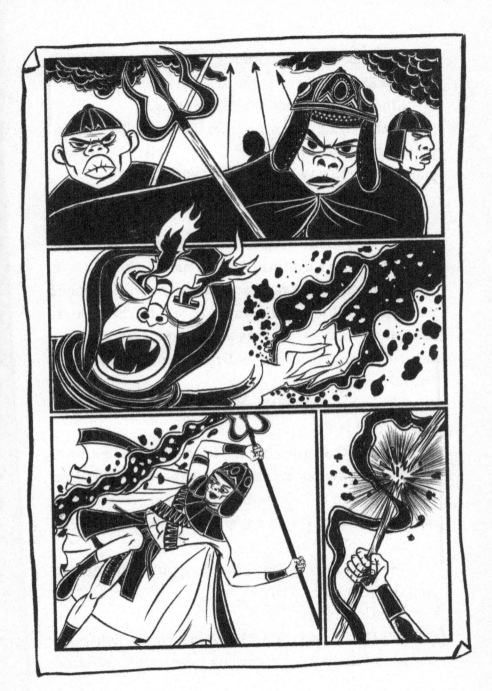

"And it looks like a toothpick?" asked Sierra.

"YEEESSSS!" Then I got worried. "Is this corny?"

"Kinda. But in a good way! Keep going."

"So that dying prince, he grabs that little sliver, transports himself down to Earth. 'Cause it's like the nearest planet, or . . . NO! WAIT! OHMYGOSH! BAM!"

Ideas were coming at me faster than I could talk.

"What?" Sierra wanted to know.

"The lady in the hospital! She's why the Doom come to Earth! 'Cause Angel ain't just her name—she's a REAL angel! Got the most pure soul in the universe! Doom needs to snatch her soul away. 'Cause if he can steal it, that pure soul energy gonna let him snuff out that last sliver of power! Then Doom will rule the universe forever! You feel me?"

Sierra was nodding. "Yeah. But where does Toothpick come into this?"

"Okay, so that prince, right? He's dying—but he knows he gotta stop the Doom from stealing that angel's soul. So he comes down to Earth with that sliver of power. But he only gets as far as this bus stop in the hood!"

"Bus stop?"

"Yeah! He's lying there, bleeding out. Fixin' to die. And this KID WALKS UP."

"And that's you?"

"YEAH! I'm just a normal kid! And I see this dude, outta nowhere. Bleeding out at my bus stop! I'm all, 'Wassup?

You need an ambulance?' And he's all, 'NO TIME FOR THAT, BOY! TAKE THIS LITTLE SLIVER! Gives you the SUPERPOWER! And you gon' NEED IT. 'Cause you gotta stop the Doom from killin' that angel! Or he gonna take over the universe!' Then, BAM! He's dead. I'm all alone! But I got the magic toothpick. And when I put it in my mouth, like a tough guy do? Turns me into a superhero! And I gotta save the universe!"

Sierra was smiling from ear to ear. "This is DOPE!"

"Right? Like, it's good?"

"Yes! You did it, Marcus! You figured the story out! That's a MOVIE."

"YAAAAAAS!"

Whole bus was staring at me, but I didn't care. I'd finally done it! Took me WEEKS of thinking, but I did it! Cracked that story open like a nut! Couldn't wait to start writing it up in the screenplay.

"Just one thing, though," said Sierra.

"What's that?"

"Giant battles in outer space? Staff of Power blowing up in a million pieces?"

"Yeah?"

"How you going to FILM that?"

CHAPTER 11

HOW YOU GOING TO FILM THAT?

This movie stuff was HARD.

I finally had THE STORY! Wrote it up in an outline. Sat my butt in the chair. Rewrote that script from top to bottom. Showed the second draft to Sierra.

She marked it all up with her bloody red notes. Then I rewrote it again.

FIFTY times!

Okay, it wasn't fifty. More like three. Maybe four.

Every time I rewrote, it got better. And every time, Sierra did a little less bleeding on it when she made her notes.

Finally, she was all, "YES! It's ready to GO!"

Then I showed it to Darren, Trish, Khalid, and my dad.

(I showed it to J.R., too. But he only read half a page.)

Every one of them was all, "YES! This screenplay SLAPS!"

That felt GREAT. And if I was making a comic? I'd be done!

But I was just getting started.

Because I had to puzzle out how to turn my superhero screenplay into a superhero MOVIE.

The thing is: When you watch a superhero movie? And they got dudes flying around? Giant battles? Stuff blowing up all over? And it looks DOPE?

That's because they spent a hundred million dollars to make it hype.

But I didn't HAVE a hundred million dollars.

I didn't even have TEN dollars.

So I had to figure out how to tell a hundred-million-dollar story . . . with zero dollars.

Sierra put me on that tip early. Whole time I was rewriting, I was changing things to make them easier to shoot.

Like Toothpick flying. Sierra was like, "I don't think so."

So I asked Darren about it in class. "Ain't you know how to do that? Don't they teach movie flying in film school?"

"For sure, brother!" Darren told me. "Just gotta put you on some wires. Shoot you against a green screen. Then fill in that background. Maybe with some drone footage."

"That cost money?"

"LOTS of money, brother!"

That's how I wound up with a walking-around Toothpick. Takes the bus when he has to. Down-to-earth kind of superhero.

Some things I just couldn't change. Like my giant battle between good and evil in the Astral Plane. It was the PERFECT opening to the movie.

But there was no way to film it for real. Ain't no Astral Plane–looking places in my neighborhood. And how was I gonna get a thousand warriors to go at it?

So I figured I'd ANIMATE it. Animation's just drawings. And if there's one thing I can do, it's draw.

I asked Khalid about it, because he was trying to make a monster movie with this kind of animation called stop-motion. The way that works, the characters are all little action figures. And you pose them just the way you want them to look in the movie.

Then you take a picture of them. Then you move them just a TINY little bit. Then you take another picture. Then you move them a tiny little bit again. Take another picture.

You do that a bunch of times, then you put all those pictures together and run them as a movie. And it looks like those action figures came to life!

That's stop-motion. Khalid had this table set up in the back of film class with these little Godzilla-looking monsters, and he was taking pictures of them. It was crazy-slow work, so he had plenty of time to talk while he was doing it.

I sat down by him and said, "Hey, Khalid. If I make the kind of animation where I just draw pictures, how many pictures I gotta draw for, like, two minutes of movie?"

"Lemme do the math," Khalid said. He whipped out his phone. Put some numbers in the calculator.

"One thousand, four hundred, and forty."

"BET!" My head just about exploded.

But then Sierra was all, "Why don't you just do a Len Burds effect?"

And I was like, "What even IS that?"

Turns out Len Burds is this dude who makes documentaries about history. Sometimes the history he's telling is so far back in the past, movies and TV weren't invented yet. So all he has for the visuals are pictures.

And if you put a still picture in a movie, that's weak. Just sits there on the screen. Audience gets bored.

But if you put up a picture and then MOVE THE CAMERA you're filming with? So you're zooming in close on one part of the picture? Or starting up close and then pulling back wide to show more of it?

That can look DOPE. And people call that the Len Burds effect.

After Sierra told me about it, I rewrote my giant space battle so I could draw the whole opening scene with just six super-dope full-page comics. Then I could give them the Len Burds treatment for the movie.

It took me some serious time to draw a half dozen super-dope pictures.

But it took a lot LESS time than drawing a THOUSAND of them.

Locations were another problem. If I couldn't find a place to film something, it had to go.

In my first draft, there was this dope sequence where Toothpick tracks the Doom across a whole bunch of rooftops.

But Sierra was all, "How many rooftops you gonna be able to film on?"

The answer was none. I can't even get on my OWN roof without going through Mr. Hampton's apartment upstairs. And Mr. Hampton ain't into that.

So in my next draft, the rooftop scenes had to go.

Same with this big fight in a subway tunnel. Wasn't going to happen.

Toothpick jumping out a skyscraper? Not in this movie.

The Doom flips over a car, then blows it up?

No, sir. Maybe in the sequel.

The only location I WOULDN'T change—no matter how many times Sierra told me to—was the hospital where the big fight happens in the climax.

"It's GOTTA be in the hospital!" I told her on the bus after she gave me notes on my fifth draft.

"How come?"

"'Cause that's where the angel's dying of the Ooze!"

"Can't she be dying at home?"

"No!"

"Why not?"

"'Cause it didn't happen that—It's not how it goes down! Angel's a nurse. Like for her job. And when the Doom makes her sick, she winds up a patient in the exact same hospital she used to work at. The other nurses are all friends with her. So they keep coming in and talking to her and crying, and it's SO SAD. . . ."

I was getting choked up just thinking about it.

"How you going to get all those actors?"

"What?"

"To play the nurses. You going to need a bunch of adults wearing nurse costumes—"

"Forget the other nurses! We don't need them. But it's GOT TO BE in a hospital."

"So where you going to film it?"

"In a hospital!"

"WHAT hospital?"

"I don't know yet! I'll figure it out."

"I'm just saying, if it's a living room—"

"IT'S A HOSPITAL!"

"Why you getting all mad?"

"'CAUSE IT'S IMPORTANT!"

My eyes wanted to cry, but I was holding them back. Sierra got the message.

"Okay. It's a hospital. Good luck finding THAT location."

Truth was, when it came to shooting the movie, ALL my locations were a problem.

'Cause Afternoon Adventures film class is at school. We can't leave the building till it's over at six. And NONE of my scenes were in a school. So I was going to have to shoot the whole thing OUT of school. On the weekends.

I was fine with that. But you can't make a movie alone.

And when I started trying to cast my movie? It got real.

"Yo, Jazmin!" I said one afternoon in film class.

"Yo, what?" she said.

"You want to be in my movie?"

"I dunno. DO I?" Jazmin was always coming with that I'm-too-good-for-you hot-girl energy. But I was used to it by now. I'd been watching how Sierra talked to Jazmin about Jazmin's part in *Phone Zombies*. So I knew the best way to handle her was to throw a lot of compliments at her.

"You'd be PERFECT for this part!" I told Jazmin. "She's an angel! But she don't even know it! Living on earth in human form. Real pretty, just like you. And she got the purest soul in the universe!"

Jazmin tried to shrug it off. But she couldn't help smiling. "Yeah, that sounds like me. When you going to shoot it? After we finish *Phone Zombies*?"

"We could do it during," I said. "'Cause the locations are all out of school. So we going to have to shoot on the weekends."

Jazmin's eyebrow shot up halfway to her hairline. "MY weekends?"

"Yeah. You good with that?"

"Pffft! You gonna pay me for my time?"

"Don't be like that! Girl, you PERFECT for this part!"

"Then you can PAY ME for it!"

"AWWW, COME ON—!"

"Boy, bye!"

I was ready to go off on Jazmin for thinking she was all that. But then Sierra smacked me in the back of the head to shut me up.

"What you hitting me for?"

"C'mere," she said. "Let's talk. It's important."

I followed Sierra to the back of the room, where nobody could hear us.

"Did Darren and Trish give you the lecture about how filmmaking's a team sport?"

I snorted. "Yeah, like a hundred times."

"Did you LISTEN?"

"Course I did! That's why I'm asking her to be in my movie!"

Sierra just rolled her eyes. "That ain't how it works, Marcus. When you on a team with someone? You in a RELATIONSHIP. And a relationship, it's like a bank account. You want something out of it? First you gotta put something INTO IT. What you ever do for Jazmin?"

"Man, she out here asking me for money—"

"'Cause you asking her for TIME! Time is money! People only got so much of it. Don't go asking a girl to show up for you until you showed up for her."

"How am I gonna show up for Jazmin? She don't want nothin' from me!"

"She trying to get her MeTube channel off the ground, ain't she? Can't you help with that?"

"What, she going to do a makeover on me? Style my hair?"

"Don't be a fool. Think of what you're good at! You could draw her up a dope title sequence! Or a logo. Use your skills to help her out."

I thought about it. "That's a good idea."

"DUH!" She rapped me on the forehead with her knuckle. Not hard enough to hurt. Just hard enough to get my attention.

"Speaking of which," she said, "did you learn your lines yet? 'Cause we fixin' to start shooting *Phone Zombies* next week. And I read a LOT of drafts of your movie. So you BETTER be bringing some game to mine."

CHAPTER 12

OTHER PEOPLE'S MOVIES

Sierra was right. I needed HELP. Not just with acting. All kinds of jobs: camera, sound, editing, effects . . . you name it.

So I had to put my own movie on hold for a minute. Build up some cred with the other kids by helping out with THEIR movies. That way, when it came time, they'd do the same for me.

Jazmin wasn't feeling it right away. When I offered to draw some dope art for her hair and makeup channel, she thought I was trying to scam her for cash. But once she saw how good the art looked—and I gave it to her FREE—she came around.

Then she asked me to draw a bunch of how-to illustrations for her. And I gotta say, that was eye-opening. If you're a boy? You have NO IDEA what goes on with girls' hair and makeup. It's A LOT. Props to those girls, man. I get tired just thinking about all the work some of them put into it.

It wasn't just Jazmin I showed up for. I drew titles for three of Amari's music videos. And when he needed somebody to wear a bunny costume in one? I played the bunny.

Not to brag, but I was a FIERCE bunny.

Except the costume was too big. So I was also a very WRINKLY bunny. Lots of sag. Especially in the legs.

Then there was Khalid. He needed HOURS of help moving those little action figures for his stop-motion project. I showed up for him. And he was glad for it. He could work twice as fast with me helping.

I was glad for it, too. 'Cause I was fixin' to hit him up for help with my Toothpick movie. And putting my time in on his stop-motion joint meant I wouldn't feel bad asking him to step up later.

But the movie that REALLY took up time was *Phone Zombies.*

Once I finally read Sierra's script, I got why Darren and Trish wanted to make it the group project. That story was TIGHT.

It was this science-fiction-horror-comedy thing where the whole school downloads a hot new gaming app on their phones. But it's a trick! Brainwashes everybody who plays it! Teachers and students both. The app controls their minds, so they just stare at their screens like zombies till it tells them to do something. Then they gotta do it.

Only two people in the whole school don't get brainwashed: this nerdy girl, Brianna, who doesn't own a phone; and this loudmouth kid, Puffer, whose phone battery's dead.

Brianna and Puffer have to figure out how to save the whole school from that evil app while the app's making all the zombies try to stop them.

Sierra played the Brianna part. I played Puffer. She'd rewritten him to be SO MUCH like me that some of what he said in the script, I'd said in real life.

Like early on, when he was talking about the evil app:

> PUFFER
> It's brainwashed them! It's like
> a North Korea phone! Gonna make
> them bow down, then blow them up
> with nuclear weapons!

> BRIANNA
> I don't think phones have nuclear
> weapons.

> PUFFER
> BET! We all gonna die in here!
> We gotta jump out the window!
> (runs over to window)
> You go first.

"You stealing from me!" I told Sierra when I read that part. "That's the same thing I said about film class!"

Sierra just shrugged. "It's a little different."

"How's it different?"

"I made it funnier."

I didn't complain too much. It was a lot easier to learn my lines when Puffer was just saying stuff I'd already said.

———

It wasn't just the script that was on point. Sierra had the whole shoot locked down.

For one thing, her scenes weren't all over the city like in my movie. Every single one was set inside the school. That meant we could shoot all of it during film class.

And when it came time to shoot a scene? Sierra knew EXACTLY what she wanted.

For every shot in the movie, she made what she called "storyboards." Those were little stick-figure drawings that showed how the shots should look. They were basic, but it didn't matter. They got the job done. When Sierra was acting in a scene, which was most of the time, she'd show the storyboards to whoever she had working the camera. That way, they knew exactly how to frame the shot, where to zoom in, and all that.

Storyboards made everything go faster and smoother. When we shot the scenes, Sierra didn't have to worry about where the camera was. She could just focus on directing the actors.

And working with people was where that girl REALLY shined.

None of us had ever acted, so we didn't know jack. But Sierra had us rehearse every scene ahead of time. And when we did something she didn't like, she always gave us a compliment before she criticized us.

I got most of my criticizing from her in the middle of the shoot. The first few days, I was just trying to act like me. And it worked, because Sierra had written Puffer to BE me.

But after a couple of days of shooting, she showed me some footage of myself.

That was a mistake. Because when I saw myself on film, I finally got what people thought was funny about me! When I'm riled up—which is MOST of the time—it's like my face turns into a cartoon. My eyebrows hit the ceiling, my eyeballs pop, my jaw drops to my chest.

No wonder people were always laughing at me when I got mad. I looked hilarious!

But then I got way too in my head about it. Started making every scene as big as I could. I'd bounce my eyebrows, bug my eyes out. Turn the volume up to eleven.

Trish called it "chewing the scenery." And Sierra had to pull me back from it.

She'd come up to me after a take and be all, "M, that is HILARIOUS! It's perfect for that scene in the hallway tomorrow! But for THIS scene . . . we need a different energy. More like 'quiet and confused.' So can you play it a little more 'Whuuuuh?' and not so much 'WHAAAAH?' Save the big stuff for later; it'll pop more. Okay? You good?"

No matter what, Sierra always stayed positive. Never blew up or yelled at anybody.

Even when folks deserved it.

Like, one super-important movie thing I never knew about is "continuity."

Continuity means everything has to be the same from one shot to the next. If your movie takes place in one day, like *Phone Zombies*, but you shoot it over TEN days? Your actors gotta look the same all ten days! Same clothes, same hair, same everything.

That's continuity.

And Jazmin was NOT good with it.

Three days into shooting, she showed up with a whole different hairstyle. Didn't matter that Sierra told her fifty times not to change her hair until the shoot was over. Jazmin went and did it anyway.

So Sierra had to reshoot a bunch of the first two days just to make Jazmin's new hair match. And she had words with Jazmin about it. But they were a WHOLE lot quieter than my words would've been.

On the bus going home, I told Sierra I couldn't believe it. "Why didn't you get hot?"

"I was! I could NOT believe that girl."

"So how come you didn't go off on her?"

"'Cause I gotta work with her the whole rest of the movie. I start beef with Jazmin now, she just going to shut down and pout. Make everything harder. I gotta stay on her good side. Keep my tiger in the cage. Case I gotta take it out later."

She never once took her tiger out of the cage. And that positive energy WORKED.

Not just on me, but everybody. Sierra made people feel GOOD. And the better they felt, the more they wanted to kick butt for her.

She got stuff out of people I never would've dreamed. She even got Officer Shirley to act in a scene! Officer Shirley's about the grumpiest woman on Earth. But she showed up. 'Cause Sierra worked her magic.

Then there were the crowd scenes, like me and Sierra sneaking down a hallway full of zombie kids staring at their phones. Or getting chased through the gym by a whole pack of zombies. Stuff like that.

When I first read the script, I thought, *This is going to look TRASH. We only got three other actors! How's she going to make Jazmin, Khalid, and Amari fill up a whole hallway?*

But Sierra got just about EVERY teacher in Afternoon Adventures—musical theater, dance, basketball, even chess club—to let their kids out of class to play movie zombies. Bunch of the teachers acted in it, too!

By the time we were done shooting, half the school was in one scene or another. And people were hyped for it. Every day, kids were coming up and asking me, "When we gonna see that movie? When Sierra gonna be done with it?"

No joke: watching what she did with that *Phone Zombies* shoot was INSPIRING.

Made me think anything was possible!

But it was scary, too. Because I wanted MY movie to be that tight.

And after watching Sierra do her thing? I didn't know if I had it in me.

CHAPTER 13

A MILLION AND ONE PROBLEMS

The whole time we were shooting *Phone Zombies*, I was trying to get *Toothpick Fights the Doom!* ready to shoot, too.

In a movie, all the stuff you have to do AFTER you write the script but BEFORE you start filming is called "preproduction."

And it is a PAIN in the butt.

You gotta go through every single scene and figure out EXACTLY what you need to shoot it: actors, equipment, props, costumes.

Then you gotta put all that stuff together.

THEN you have to make a schedule. Figure out how much time you need for each scene, where the locations are, what time of day it is, which actors gotta be there, how the weather will be if you shoot outside, whether you got enough light. . . .

It was A LOT.

And I'm not what you'd call "good at organizing stuff."

So when I sat down and tried to figure out everything I needed, I just about had a nervous breakdown.

Trish told me to make a list to keep track of it all. So I did. This was my list:

- draw battle scenes
- make script copies
- Toothpick costume? (cape/boots/shirt?)
- Prince Ka costume?
- Doom costume?
- Genie costume?
- cast Victims 1 and 2 (Khalid/Amari?)
- beg Jazmin to play Angel
- cast Prince Ka (Darren?)
- make J.R. read script for Doom
- get camera (Darren/Trish?)
- get sound gear
- get toothpicks (diner?)
- make Ooze
- make finger spears
- music?
- schedule
- ride bus Sat am—how crowded? Ok to shoot?
- check w/ actors re: weekends
- street scenes—which streets? Time of day?
- find nicer apt for int. (Khalid?)
- find HOSPITAL???

- storyboards?
- rehearse actors—when? (J.R.?)

Once I had the list, I started trying to cross items off of it.

Some of them were easy, like getting the other kids to be actors. After I'd helped them with their projects, even Jazmin was willing to show up for me. But they all had other stuff to do on the weekends, so when it came time to make a schedule, I'd have to work around all that.

Khalid helped me figure out the Ooze. That's the black death gunk that leaks out of people's mouths when the Doom attacks 'em.

Only thing I could think to use for the Ooze was hot tar.

But making actors put hot tar in their mouths? That seemed like a bad idea.

Plus, I didn't know where to get hot tar.

So I asked Khalid what he'd do, because he seemed like the kind of dude who'd be into making stuff like Ooze.

I was right about that. Took him about two seconds to figure it out.

"That's easy, dawg! Grape jelly and black food coloring."

I already had grape jelly in the fridge. And Dad bought me the food coloring. So that took care of the Ooze.

Figuring out Toothpick's finger spears was harder. I tried to make some out of chopsticks and construction paper.

That did NOT look good.

Then I remembered one of Jazmin's MeTube tutorials

was about doing your own acrylic nails. She'd glued these three-inch-long, bright yellow with pink polka-dot extensions on all ten of her fingernails.

Next time I saw her in class, I said, "Yo! Jazmin! Think you could make me finger spears? Like, some long black razor-sharp extensions?"

Her eyes lit up. "Oooooh! You want to rock STILETTO nails!"

"That sounds right. Can you hook me up?"

"I dunno. It's a lot. You go to a salon, they gonna charge you forty bucks for that."

"You ain't gonna charge me, are you? I did all that art for you!"

"And I'm gonna act in your movie! But acrylics cost actual MONEY, Marcus." She got a wicked grin on her face. "Although I guess I could front you . . . if you let me shoot it for a stiletto-nails tutorial on my channel."

"You want to do MY nails on YOUR MeTube?"

"Heck, yeah! I'll make you a STAR! You be a fashion diva!"

"Ain't nobody want to watch that!" I told her.

"I'D watch that," said Amari.

"I'd DEFINITELY watch that," Khalid added. "That could go VIRAL."

"Oh, man! Seriously?" I didn't want to spend the rest of my life getting clowned on 'cause I got my nails done on MeTube.

"Or you could just pay me for it," said Jazmin.

I needed those finger spears. And I was dead broke. So I said yes.

Then I had to figure out how to schedule all the scenes where Toothpick rocks his finger spears into just one Saturday. Otherwise, I'd have to go to school all week wearing the stiletto nails. That'd be even worse than a MeTube video.

The more items I knocked off the list, the harder it got.

Darren didn't want to play Prince Ka. That's the dude who comes down to Earth and dies right after he gives Marko Jackson the magic toothpick.

"I need an adult!" I told Darren. "If I cast a kid, it's gonna look corny!"

"I hear you, brother. But you're filming on a WEEKEND."

"So?"

"Weekends are Darren Time," said Darren.

"Don't be like that, Darren! Ain't you all about helping me make my dreams come true?"

"ABSOLUTELY, brother! From three to six on weekdays."

I figured with enough sweet talking, I MIGHT be able to get Darren to change his mind about showing up on a Saturday.

But what I definitely COULDN'T talk him or Trish into was letting me use the camera and sound equipment.

"We just can't do it, Marcus," Trish told me. "That equipment's property of Afternoon Adventures. It's only for use in school."

Didn't matter what I said to Darren and Trish. It was a hard no. They were NEVER going to let me borrow that equipment.

And no camera meant no movie.

It wasn't just the camera. I couldn't figure out what to do for costumes, either. Where was I going to get a Grim Reaper cloak for the Doom? I thought the theater department at school might have one. But after my day in musical theater class, that drama teacher had beef with me.

So I was STUCK.

The more I tried to think my way through it, the more stressed I got. It got so bad that when Dad came home after work one night, I was curled up on the floor like a baby.

"What's the matter? You got another bellyache?"

"Can't get my movie made, Dad! It's all falling apart!"

"Come eat this turkey wrap. We'll talk it out."

Over dinner, I laid out all my issues for Dad. He tried to be helpful.

"Ain't your phone got a camera in it? Can't you use that?"

"My battery's trash! Lasts like three minutes! I'd have to recharge it after every take!"

"Somebody else got a phone camera? How about that smart girl? Always knows what to do?"

"Sierra? She's busy with her own movie," I said.

But that got me thinking.

I stayed up half the night thinking. Because I could maybe see a solution. But it was a big decision. And I didn't know if I wanted to go down that road.

When Sierra got on the bus the next morning, I'd planned out exactly what I wanted to say.

"You know how filmmaking's a team sport?" I asked.

"Yeah?"

"I've been thinking about my team for *Toothpick*. And I don't want to just play minor league ball. I want a championship! I want a Super Bowl–winning movie! You feel me?"

"Uh-huh. It's a lot of swagger. But okay."

"And you can't win a Super Bowl with one dude playing all the positions."

"Taylor Berry can."

"Maybe. But I ain't Taylor Berry! I'm like . . . a running back. But I need a quarterback! So what would you say . . . about being my quarterback?"

"I'm playing Genie already," Sierra reminded me. Genie is Toothpick's sidekick. Comes down to Earth to show him how to use his magic powers and whatnot.

"But Genie ain't the quarterback," I said. "Don't you want to be the quarterback?"

"I don't know," she said. "This is a real confusing metaphor. What's a quarterback supposed to be in this movie?"

"The director!"

"You want ME to direct YOUR movie?"

"Yeah!"

She narrowed her eyes. "Is this 'cause Darren and Trish won't let you borrow the camera, but you figure they'd let ME borrow it?"

Dang!

This girl was SMART.

"It's a little of that," I told her. "But it's other stuff, too! I need costumes. But that drama teacher hates me! And if I gotta work with actors and they're stinking it up? Gonna drive me nuts! I'm going to blow my top and yell at them. Get everybody mad. But you're GOOD at that stuff! I ain't! I need help."

Sierra pulled her head back like she was surprised. "Ain't this a thing? You come a long way, Marcus! It's like I'm watching you grow as a person."

"Don't be clowning me like that! You want to do it or not?"

She thought it over.

Then she shook her head. "No. I ain't into that."

OUCH.

I felt like my stomach went straight through the floor of that bus and got run over by the wheels.

Then Sierra cracked a grin.

"I'm just messing with you. I'll do it."

"WHY'D YOU DO THAT TO ME?"

"Thought it'd be funny. Make your eyes bug out. But it wasn't funny. It was sad! Don't make that face again."

"DON'T MESS WITH ME LIKE THAT AGAIN!"

This girl had been directing my movie all of three seconds. And I was already thinking it was the worst mistake of my life.

But it was too late. We were in it now.

CHAPTER 14

WE'RE DOING THIS!

I watched the whole thing go down. And I STILL can't tell you how Sierra finessed that camera out of Darren and Trish.

It was the end of film class on the day after we finished shooting *Phone Zombies*. The other kids were all walking out. Sierra turned to me and said, "Follow along. Stand right behind me. And DON'T open your mouth."

Then she walked up to Darren and Trish and was like, "Heeeey, sooo, guuuys? I don't want to get all mushy? But the two of you been SUCH a help with *Phone Zombies* that I just want to say THANK YOU . . . for CHANGING MY LIFE."

When they heard that, man? Darren and Trish just about died of happiness. The next couple of minutes were embarrassing. 'Cause it was like a love-in, and I wasn't invited. I just had to stand there looking a fool while the three of them gushed at each other.

Then—so slow and smooth they never saw it coming—Sierra changed the subject from "Ain't it great what we did together?" to "So, what are we doing NEXT?"

And Darren and Trish were like, "Girl, we GOT YOUR BACK on your next movie! Whatever you need! Just say the word!"

And Sierra was all, "Actuuuuallyyyyyy . . . can I borrow your camera equipment the Saturday after next?"

Then it was all over. Except for the arguing between Darren and Trish over who was going to show up on Saturday with the equipment. They wouldn't let it out of their sight, so one of them had to go along and babysit it.

Darren lost, because Trish is just smarter than he is.

And once he got stuck with babysitting the camera and the microphone, Darren said yes to playing Prince Ka, too.

Then he asked us how many Saturdays we'd need to shoot the movie.

I said, "Probably three," because that was the truth.

That's when I found out why Sierra told me not to open my mouth.

'Cause me telling Darren we wanted THREE Saturdays from him just about blew up the whole thing.

So I had to shut up again while Sierra promised Darren we'd get it done in two.

Problem with that was, we'd been making the schedule. And it seemed IMPOSSIBLE to shoot *Toothpick Fights the Doom!* in just two Saturdays.

But Sierra told me not to worry. Said we'd cross that bridge when we came to it.

The next day, she worked the same kind of magic with the musical theater teacher. Got us a Grim Reaper cloak for the Doom and this pharaoh-looking outfit for Darren.

The Toothpick costume, I had to make myself. In my comics, Toothpick wears the usual superhero getup. Form-fitting space-age fabrics and whatnot.

Movie Toothpick wears a T-shirt. But it's a DOPE T-shirt! Long sleeve, size too small so it fits real snug. Got a Toothpick logo I drew on the chest. Pairs up good with my sweatpants. Those are TWO sizes too small. But that's good! If you don't get too close, you can't even tell they're sweatpants.

The rest of preproduction just flew by. There were a million things to do, and I had to do most of them. But it was pretty smooth sailing.

Except for the fights I got into with Sierra.

Biggest one was over storyboards. She asked me to draw 'em up. But she didn't like the way I was framing some of the shots. And she was all kinds of stressed. Because on top of the preproduction for *Toothpick*, she was trying to edit *Phone Zombies*, add Amari's music to it, and get it all done in time for the Fall Arts Showcase. Which was in two weeks.

I guess that was a lot. 'Cause when Sierra looked at my storyboards for *Toothpick*, she wasn't her usual never-get-mad-at-anybody self. She was on a REAL short fuse.

"This ain't what I told you to do!"

"But this is how it looks in my comic!"

"This ain't your comic! It's a movie!"

"Yeah—it's a movie . . . of my comic!"

"Marcus! Do it the way I told you!"

"Don't go ordering me! You ain't my boss!"

"I'm the DIRECTOR! You want me to direct? Or argue with you? 'Cause I ain't here to do both!"

"Then let me do it right!"

"It's right when I SAY it's right!"

"Don't get hot, you two," Trish called out from across the room.

"Filmmaking's a team sport!" Darren reminded us.

"Heck, yeah, it's a team," Sierra told him. "And I'M the quarterback! This little dude here—"

"DON'T CALL ME LITTLE!"

"—he's just a running back! And the fool's going downfield on a pass pattern when he's supposed to be blocking behind the line!"

I never should've told her she was quarterback. 'Cause she shoved that back in my face every time we fought. Also, it turned out she knew a lot more about football than I did.

It wasn't too bad, though. We only fought seven or eight more times over the storyboards.

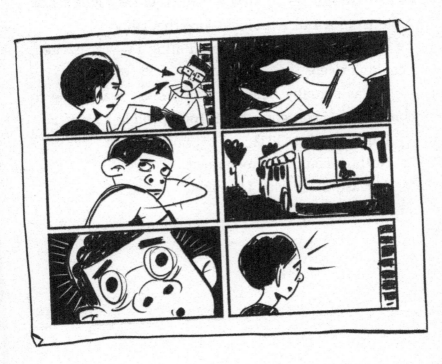

She quit after two of them.

But only for a couple of minutes.

And I think it was mostly 'cause she was so stressed about getting *Phone Zombies* finished in time to show it at the Fall Arts Showcase.

But busy as she was? The Friday before we started filming *Toothpick*, she still took time out to rehearse the scenes we were going to shoot the next day.

It went great! We had all the actors except J.R. He didn't want to quit playing basketball and come over to the filmmaking class to rehearse.

That was fine, though. In that first day of scenes, all he had to do as the Doom was stand there and look scary. A piece of furniture could've done that job.

The night before we started filming, I was so excited, I couldn't sleep.

It was actually happening! My story was going to come to life! I was going to BE Toothpick! In a MOVIE!

We were DOING IT!

Nothing could go wrong now!

At least, that's what I thought.

CHAPTER 15

FIRST DAY OF SHOOTING!

Here's what I learned about making movies: no matter how hard you try, or how much you do to get ready? Something's going to go wrong.

And on the first day of *Toothpick Fights the Doom!*, that something was J.R.

We were starting super-early because we had a LOT of shooting to do. The opening scene—when I'm headed to school, and I find Prince Ka dying on the sidewalk across from my bus stop—takes place first thing in the morning. So we wanted to shoot it right after sunrise to get the light just so.

I was out of bed at six. By six-fifteen, I was standing outside J.R.'s door with a bag full of costumes and whatnot, waiting for him to come out.

But he wasn't coming out.

I texted him. No answer.

Texted him again. Nothing.

Called him. Didn't pick up.

Then I had to shut my phone off. 'Cause the battery was down to fifteen percent, and I had a long day ahead of me.

I didn't want to knock on J.R.'s front door on account of his mom.

She is NOT a morning person. She ain't friendly even in the afternoons.

But I couldn't help it. My whole movie was at stake here!

So I knocked.

Nobody answered.

Knocked again.

Then again.

And again.

FINALLY, the door opened.

But it wasn't J.R.

It was J.R.'s mom.

You ever see somebody who's tired and angry at the same time? Like, they're "tangry"?

That was J.R.'s mom. That woman was TANGRY.

And I got an earful from her.

Eventually, she got tired of yelling at me and went to J.R.'s room to yell at him, too.

That at least got him out of bed and standing up.

"Just lemme get a shower," he told me.

"You kidding me? We gotta GO! They're waiting for us!"

"Need a shower, fam!"

"The Doom don't shower! He's a supervillain! Stinks it up!"

"Gotta shower, fam. Wakes me up."

"There's no TIME!"

"I'll meet you there."

I didn't want to keep arguing and set his mom off again. Plus, we were shooting just a couple of blocks away. And we didn't need him till the end of the scene. We could do the first few shots without him.

So I left him there to shower. Headed for the bus stop.

I was the first one there. That got me scared: *What if nobody shows up?*

But Sierra rolled in a couple of minutes later.

"Where's your boy at?"

"He'll be here. Had to take a shower first."

She snorted. "Doom don't need no shower."

"That's what I said!"

Then Darren showed up with the camera equipment. A minute after that, Khalid and Amari came by. Khalid was going to work the camera, and Amari was doing sound.

While we were setting up, my heart started flapping like a bird.

I was NERVOUS!

But it went great. Darren was an awesome Prince Ka. And that grape jelly with food coloring was PERFECT for the Ooze dribbling out his mouth.

Except nobody brought paper towels. So Darren had to sort of lick the Ooze off when we were done. He wasn't too happy about that.

Pretty soon, all we had left to shoot at the bus stop was the Doom.

In the script, after Prince Ka gives me the magic

toothpick and dies, his body just disappears! Trips me out! But I don't know what to do. So I just cross the street. Get on the city bus and ride off to school.

The way we storyboarded it, when that bus pulls away . . . THE DOOM is standing across the street! Out of nowhere! Right where Prince Ka disappeared!

Amari said he could come up with some scary music to make it super-creepy.

It was going to be PERFECT. Except we couldn't shoot it without the Doom.

And J.R. was nowhere in sight.

I used Sierra's phone to text him. No answer.

So I ran home to get him.

Had to do some more knocking.

Then take some more yelling from his mom. Finally, I got myself into J.R.'s room.

The fool was still lyin' in bed! He'd gone back to sleep!

I couldn't even. I went OFF!

Practically kicked that boy down the street to the bus stop.

J.R. wasn't too happy at that point. Nobody was.

Then we put that Grim Reaper cloak on him for the Doom costume.

It was the first time we'd seen him wear it.

And it was EVERY KIND OF WRONG.

He looked like a shorty in a Halloween costume three sizes too big!

Sierra busted up laughing. "Oh, that is PERFECT."

I blew my top. "WHAT YOU MEAN?"

"It's hilarious!"

"IT AIN'T SUPPOSED TO BE! That's THE DOOM! HE'S A SUPERVILLAIN!"

Amari and Khalid were laughing, too.

"Look more like BABY Villain to me," Amari said.

I was so spun out, my whole body was starting to shake.

J.R. took his Doom hood off. Still looked about half awake.

"Y'all got any breakfast food?"

My own breakfast was fixin' to wind up on the sidewalk. We had a serious problem. And if I didn't do something about it, my whole movie was going to be ruined.

CHAPTER 16

HOW TO FIRE YOUR BEST FRIEND

"It's just WRONG!"

Sierra and I were standing a few feet down the sidewalk from the others, having an emergency conversation. I was trying not to yell.

"I dunno." Sierra shrugged. "If we're making a comedy—"

"This ain't a comedy! It's a SUPERHERO movie! With a SUPERVILLAIN!"

"But we agreed it's going to be funny—"

"Not THIS kind of funny! That's THE DOOM! Gotta be big! Mean! Scary! Tryin' to rule the universe! Not trippin' over his robe!"

Sierra took another look back down the street at J.R. The bottom of the Doom cloak was bunched up on the sidewalk around his shoes. He was munching a bag of carrots, because the only food anybody brought was Darren's healthy snacks.

"I guess we could try to put some platform heels on

him?" Sierra said. "Then maybe stuff some padding on his shoulders."

"No. No. No!" I was getting sick to my stomach just thinking about how trash that'd look. "It's just WRONG. We gotta recast him! Get a whole new Doom."

"And lose a day of filming?"

My stomach flipped at that, too. "How many shots he in today?"

"Let me count." Sierra looked over the notebook where we'd written down all the shots we'd planned for day one. "Actually . . ."

"What?"

"It ain't too bad. Like six or seven. And mostly he's just supposed to stand there and look evil. So we can skip those. Add in another scene from next week to fill out the day. Then pick up all the Doom shots later."

"Let's do it. But who we going to get to replace him? Who's going to play the Doom?"

"Figure that out once you solve the first problem," said Sierra.

"What's the first problem?"

"Telling J.R. he's fired."

"Why do I gotta do it? Dude's my best friend!"

"That's why! He's YOUR dawg. You want to put him down? Ain't nobody but you pulling that trigger."

"Aw, man!"

That walk back over to J.R. was the longest fifty feet of my life.

I mean, yeah—he'd done me dirty with the sleeping in and not wanting to rehearse. And I don't think he EVER got around to reading the script.

But he was my best friend! There from the beginning! First person who ever read my Toothpick comics! First person I ever told about the movie. First person I cast in it!

And he had his heart set on being the Doom. He was going to be SO SAD!

I didn't want him taking it wrong. Thinking I got a big head. Turning my back on my boy.

Maybe I could find another part for him. Rewrite the script. Make up a whole other character just for J.R.

Yeah! That was the way to play this!

I'd almost reached him by then. He was still chewing on Darren's carrots.

"Why ain't we started yet, fam? This going to take all day!"

"Yo, dude—can we talk for a sec? In private?"

He gave a shrug. Picked up the hem of his Doom cloak so he wouldn't trip over it while we walked down the sidewalk to be alone.

I took a deep breath. I knew this was going to hurt.

"Here's the thing, dude. You're my brother! I love you! And I ALWAYS got your back. For life! And I want you in this movie! But Sierra and I been talking—y'know, she's the director, so, like, you know how it is—and the Doom is, like, kinda maybe not EXACTLY the right part for you—"

"I ain't gotta do this?"

"Not 'cause you're bad at it! Only 'cause—"

J.R. already had that Doom cloak all the way up over his head to get it off.

"Dang! I coulda slept in, fam! Here you go—"

He handed me the cloak like it was hot.

"Don't worry!" I told him. "I'll write you another part—"

"No! Don't sweat that. It's all good, fam. If I knew you had to get up this early to make movies? I mean, dang!"

"I guess I could schedule you later in the day—"

"No, no! It's all good! One thing, though—"

"Yeah?"

"Can I borrow your GameBox? While you shooting the movie?"

"I guess so?"

"You're my boy!" He gave me dap. And it was HAPPY dap. With a big old smile. Like he just won the lottery. "I'll go tell your dad it's cool if I take the GameBox down to my place. Catch you later!"

J.R. tore down that street like he was shot out a cannon.

So in the end?

That whole "firing my best friend" thing went a LOT better than I expected.

It went a little TOO well, to be honest.

CHAPTER 17

NEED A NEW DOOM!

After J.R. left, the first day of filming went fine. We shot all the scenes on our schedule except for one.

It was supposed to be on a city bus. But Darren made some noise about how we couldn't film on the bus without a permit from the city. That seemed whack to me, because the bus was empty, and the driver didn't care. But Darren did. So no bus scene.

Sierra told me not to worry about it. She said we'd figure it out later. And in the scenes we DID shoot, she crushed it playing my sidekick, Genie.

I thought I did pretty good as Marko Jackson, the normal kid who turns into Toothpick. But I wasn't sure, because Sierra wouldn't let me watch any of the footage. She said she didn't want me getting all up in my own head like I did on *Phone Zombies*.

I was glad I'd asked her to direct, so I wouldn't have to think about stuff like that. My head was full already.

All I could think that whole day—and the whole NEXT day—was WHO'S GOING TO PLAY THE DOOM?

True fact: a superhero movie without a good villain is trash. Whoever played the Doom had to be GREAT.

And not just great. LARGE. In my comics, the Doom is huge! He's ten feet tall! Built like a ton of bricks!

I couldn't think of ANYBODY I knew who was big like that. Except my uncle Terry.

But when I ran that idea by Dad at dinner on Sunday, he squashed it.

"The thing with Uncle Terry . . ." Dad shook his head, all slow and thoughtful. "He ain't real good at showing up for stuff. Especially before noon."

I'd had enough of people who couldn't wake up in the morning. So I didn't want to ask Uncle Terry unless I was desperate.

By Monday morning, though? I was getting REAL close to desperate. I'd been thinking on it two whole days. And besides Uncle Terry, there was only one person I knew who even LOOKED like he could be a supervillain.

The trouble was, he was an ACTUAL villain.

"Think of anybody for the Doom?" Sierra asked me as soon as she got on the bus that morning.

"Kinda?"

"What's that mean?"

"Means I thought of somebody . . . but it's a BAD idea."

"Who is it?"

"I ain't even telling you."

"Why not?"

"'Cause what if you think it's a good idea?"

"Don't be a fool. Who is it?"

I took a deep breath. Once I said it, I couldn't UN-say it. Sierra was getting mad. "C'mon! Spill!"

"Tyrell."

Her eyes turned saucer-size. "Big Tyrell? Ain't he in jail?"

"Nah. He got sent away. But he been back a while now."

She was quiet for a second, thinking it over.

"He's actually perfect," she said.

"I can't ask him!" I told her. "He'll just beat me down! Steal all my money!"

She gave me side-eye. "You ain't got no money to steal."

"Tyrell don't know that!"

"Whatever. I'm the director. I'LL ask him."

"What if he robs YOU?"

She thought about it for a bit. "I'll ask him in the hallway. Between classes. He ain't gonna run me in front of teachers."

"He might."

She sighed. "I can't believe I'm doing this. It ain't even my movie."

———

That whole day, I was nervous just thinking about Sierra asking Tyrell to play the Doom. When she came into film class, first thing I did was ask how it went.

"I don't know," she said.

"You didn't ask him?"

"No, I asked him."

"What'd he say?"

"Said he wanted to read the script."

"What'd you do?"

"What do you think? I gave him the script!"

That sounded bad. Tyrell didn't seem like a reading-the-script kind of dude. I was worried he took it just so he could roll it up and beat me on the head with it next time he saw me.

When film class ended, Sierra and I went out to the bus stop. Tyrell and three of his crew were waiting for us. Sure enough, he had my script all rolled up to beat me with.

"Yo, Little Man!" He pointed at me with the rolled-up script.

My stomach started to flip-flop.

"Just be cool," Sierra whispered to me.

"I'm going to run," I whispered back.

"Don't!" She grabbed my arm so I couldn't run.

Then Tyrell was standing over me, blotting out the light.

"You write this script?" His voice was like booming thunder.

"Yeah . . . ?" My voice was like baby tinkle.

"You playing the Toothpick? That gonna be you?"

"Maybe?"

He raised up the script.

This was it, man. I was gonna DIE! Tyrell was gonna smack me to death with my own script!

But he didn't smack me. He just opened it up and pointed to a page. He'd written all over it in chicken-scratch pencil.

"I got some notes on my character."

CHAPTER 18

TYRELL HAS SOME NOTES

Twenty minutes later, Sierra and I were sitting in Burger World across from Tyrell and three of his crew—Sly, Naz, and Double D.

Tyrell was explaining why we needed to put all three of them in the movie.

"They can be thugs, see? Like maybe the Doom gets in their brains, and he be mind-controlling them. So they try to run little Marko. But then Little Man here—" He pointed at me. "You turn into Toothpick! Beat these thugs down!"

"Sooooo . . ." Sierra was talking all slow and careful. Like she was walking through a minefield and didn't want to step wrong or she'd blow herself up. "The reason . . . for adding all that . . . to the movie . . . would be . . . ?"

"It's a build-up!" Tyrell told her. "To the hospital scene! 'Cause that's like the boss battle, right? But you can't have no boss battle if you don't take down some small fry first."

Sly, Naz, and Double D all made faces when Tyrell called them small fry.

And they weren't small at all! They were BIG! Except
Tyrell was even BIGGER.

Sierra was nodding. "I feel that. It's a good note!" She
looked at me. "Can you rewrite the script? Put in a new
fight sequence?"

"Yeah," I said. "Sounds dope."

The thought of me beating all those dudes down in
the movie made my heart thump. 'Cause if they forgot
we were acting? They could put some serious hurt on me.

But it really COULD be dope if they actually let me
beat them down.

And there was NO WAY I could say no to a note from Tyrell. That dude could chew me up for breakfast, poop me out for lunch, and not even notice.

"You got any other notes?" Sierra asked him.

"Yeah," he said. "Doom needs a catchphrase. Something hype! Like, 'THE WORLD IS MINE!'"

"But the Doom don't talk," I said.

It was true. In all my comics, the Doom never says a word. He's a silent killer!

But this was one of those times when my mouth gets WAY ahead of my brain.

Because Tyrell is ALSO a silent killer.

And when I told him the Doom don't talk? He gave me a LOOK.

The kind that turns your insides to jelly.

I started babbling. "Yeah!—no!—that!—good!—CATCHPHRASE! LET'S DO IT!"

Then I think I passed out for a second. Next thing I knew, everybody was nodding like Tyrell playing the Doom was a done deal.

"And you're okay to shoot the next few Saturdays?" Sierra asked him.

Tyrell nodded. "I'll make time." Then he looked over at me. "You gonna get on that rewrite, Little Man?"

"You know it!" My voice squeaked when I said it.

"And you're all good with the hospital scene?" Sierra asked Tyrell.

I gave her side-eye. *Why's she asking about the hospital scene?*

Tyrell nodded. "Yeah. It's tight."

"'Cause we ain't got a hospital room to shoot it in," she said. "So it's probably gonna have to get rewritten—"

"Aww, not this again!"

"Marcus, I'm *telling* you—"

Sierra and I were fixin' to get into it for the millionth time. But then Tyrell shut us both up.

"I can get you a hospital room," he said.

"What now?" Sierra and I quit arguing to stare at him.

For half a second, I was scared he meant he could PUT ME in a hospital room.

"All you gotta do is walk in," he told us. "Find an empty room and shoot in it."

"I don't . . . think . . . that's . . . a . . ." Sierra was doing her slow-talking thing again.

"Naw, it's good!" he said. "I went to this hospital last week to visit my cousin? 'Cause his leg was busted up? Long as you got a room number? Look like you know where you're going? They just let you stroll right in. And some of them rooms is empty! We can go in first thing in the morning. Shoot it and split. Boom, boom, bam."

"LET'S DO IT!" I was so happy to hear that, I just about jumped out of my seat.

"Huh . . . yeah . . . well . . . that's an option . . . ," Sierra said.

"That's NOT an option!" Sierra yelled.

"Why not?"

We were on the bus going home. She was unloading everything she didn't want to say in front of Tyrell and his boys.

"Marcus! You can't just walk into a hospital, grab a room, and start shooting! There's no way that's legal!"

"But it ain't, like, *illegal* illegal," I said. "It's more like . . . maybe slightly wrong."

She crossed her arms, like *nuh-uh*. "Not in a million years are we doing this."

"Can't we just try it?" I asked her. "What do we got to lose?"

"You think Darren's going to let us shoot a FIGHT SCENE in a hospital we're not even supposed to BE in? That brother lost his mind when we wanted to film two people talking in the back of a bus!"

"Oh, man . . . !"

I'd forgotten about Darren. Sierra was right. As long as he was hanging around babysitting the camera, there was NO WAY we were going to shoot wild in a hospital.

"If we just change the location—" Sierra started to say.

"We're NOT changing it!"

Sierra scrunched up her face. "But WHY? I still don't get it. Why's the hospital such a big deal—"

"IT JUST IS!"

Folks at the front of the bus were turning around to stare at us. I lowered my voice.

"You don't understand! Okay? It's just . . . I NEED IT in the movie."

It was the truth.

I HAD to save that Angel in the hospital. It was the whole point! Always had been.

Sierra sighed. "Okay. But we can't just walk in. So how we going to—"

"I'll figure it out! We don't gotta shoot the hospital scene till the week after next."

"So we gonna shoot that whole new fight scene THIS weekend? You gonna get that rewrite done in time?"

"Oh, man!" I had more work to do.

Making a movie was just work on top of work.

CHAPTER 19

SECOND DAY OF SHOOTING!

I didn't get much sleep that week.

'Cause first, I had to stay up late to get the rewrite done.

Then the next night, I had to stay up late to do the rewrite of the rewrite, after Sierra read it and gave me notes.

And the night after THAT was the rewrite of the rewrite of the rewrite. 'Cause when Tyrell read it, he had some notes, too.

He was all kinds of picky about how the script should be. And going into that next Saturday, I was all kinds of WORRIED he was going to stink up the joint.

But he CRUSHED it! Dude was TERRIFYING! Brought the Doom to life!

He was so huge, when he put on that big Grim Reaper cloak, the bottom didn't touch the ground anymore. You could see Tyrell's Jordans peeking out from under it!

Sierra had to frame the shots to keep his Jordans out of the picture. Didn't seem right for the Master of Evil . . . from the Astral Plane . . . to be wearing high-tops.

Other than that, Tyrell was PERFECT.

And that whole second Saturday of shooting *Toothpick Fights the Doom!* was straight-up MAGIC.

It wasn't just because of Tyrell. It was also because Darren left early. So early, he practically wasn't even there.

The second location we went to that day was this little park near school. That's where we were going to do the scene where Marko first meets his sidekick, Genie. We'd WANTED to shoot it the week before, on the city bus, which made a thousand times more sense than a park bench. But Darren wouldn't let us 'cause we didn't have a permit, blah blah blah.

We were just getting ready to shoot when Darren pulled Sierra and me aside.

"I got a BIG problem," he said.

My stomach hit the ground when I heard that. I was thinking, *What now? We barely started!*

But it turned out to be good news.

"I just got a text from the restaurant." Darren waited tables on Saturday nights. "Somebody got sick, and they need me to work a double today."

"So when you gotta leave?" Sierra asked him.

"Like . . . now."

"But we got a whole day of shooting to do!"

Darren made a face like he was torn up. "I know! And here's the thing: if you SWEAR to me you won't let ANYTHING happen to that equipment—"

"'Course not!" Sierra told him.

"And don't tell ANYBODY I left you alone with it—"

"Hundred percent!" I promised. "Not a soul!"

"'Cause I could SERIOUSLY lose my job if something happens to that camera—"

"Nothing will happen to it! I swear," said Sierra. "We'll guard it with our lives."

"And not a word! Even to Trish. ESPECIALLY to Trish."

"Totally!" I told him. "We got you!"

"You sure?"

"Absolutely!" Sierra said.

"On the soul of my great-grammy!" I promised.

Darren nodded. "Okay. I'll text you tomorrow to get the camera back. Good luck! Have a great shoot!"

Then he tore off to go to work. We watched him go.

I looked at Sierra. She had a little smile on her face.

"So this scene in the park . . . ?" I said.

"Yeah?"

"Be a WHOLE lot better if we could shoot it on the bus." She nodded. "It would."

"And it's still early," I said. "Bus gonna be empty."

"I bet it will."

"So what you think we should do?"

She thought about it for a second. "We probably shouldn't shoot on the bus."

"We're gonna, though, right?"

Sierra nodded. "Yeah, we are."

We shot that scene in three takes on an empty bus, and it was DOPE.

The rest of the day was off the hook. I got to act like I was beating down three of the scariest dudes in my whole school! AND I got my nails done.

When it was time to put the finger spears on so I could shoot the big new fight scene with Sly, Naz, and

Double D, we all went over to Jazmin's apartment and filmed her putting the black stiletto nails on me for her MeTube channel.

The best part of that was Jazmin let us use the tutorial as a movie promo. She introduced me as "Marcus Jenkins, star of the MAJOR MOTION PICTURE *Toothpick Fights the Doom!*"

Then Naz yelled, "Coming soon!"

Sly was all, "In theaters everywhere!"

Double D went, "And introducing . . . Tyrell Witherspoon as THE DOOM!"

When D said that, Khalid whipped the camera over to Tyrell, who was wearing his Doom cloak and looking super-scary.

It was awesome. Then Jazmin did my nails.

She actually wound up getting THREE vids for her channel that day instead of one. 'Cause halfway through the big fight scene—which we shot on this dead-end street a couple of blocks from Sierra's place—I snagged a nail on Naz's jacket, and it broke off.

That was my bad. I just wasn't used to having three-inch acrylics on the ends of my fingers.

So I had to ask Jazmin to fix it. And she was all, "Get that camera over here! This is CONTENT!"

That's how we ended up shooting an emergency "How to Fix a Busted Acrylic Nail" video right there on the street.

And we turned that into ANOTHER movie-promo collab.

Then at the END of the day, when we were done shooting all the Toothpick stuff, we went back to Jazmin's and shot a "How to REMOVE Your Acrylic Nails" video.

By the time Sierra and I left Jazmin's to go home, it was after dark.

I was bone-tired. But it was a GOOD tired.

We'd shot most of the movie by then. The only really big scene we didn't have yet was the climax in the hospital. We still had no clue where to shoot that, but at least we'd talked Darren into one more day of filming.

As Sierra and I walked down the street in the dark,

lugging Darren's equipment, I realized something: we were A LOT closer to finished than we were to starting.

Sooner or later, *Toothpick Fights the Doom!* was going to be an ACTUAL MOVIE.

Just the thought of it gave me a flutter in my stomach.

"You think it's going to be good?" I asked Sierra.

"What, the *Toothpick* movie?" she said.

"Yeah, the *Toothpick* movie! What you think I'm talking about?"

"We got a whole OTHER movie coming out this week," she reminded me.

That was *Phone Zombies.* Thursday evening was the Afternoon Adventures Fall Arts Showcase, and Sierra's movie was going to close out the night.

When she mentioned it, that flutter in my belly turned into a full-on storm. The arts showcase draws a CROWD. Half the school and a whole lot of parents were going to watch me act in *Phone Zombies.*

I didn't know how to feel about that.

Excited, for sure.

But scared, too.

"What if it stinks?" I asked Sierra.

"Which one?"

"Both of them!"

She shook her head. "Don't sweat that. *Phone Zombies* is DOPE. *Toothpick* will be, too."

"How do you know? We ain't even done shooting!"

"Trust me," she said. "We got some GOLD today. Soon as I finish editing *Phone Zombies*, I'll make a rough cut of *Toothpick* so you can see what we got."

Hearing that just made me even more scared and excited.

What if it all worked out great, and I blew up? Like a rock star!

Or what if it didn't? And I just looked a fool in front of everybody?

Or what if it was neither? What if we did all this work—and nobody cared?

Tired as I was, I didn't know how I'd get myself to sleep the next few nights. My head was just buzzing too hard.

CHAPTER 20

THE WORLD PREMIERE OF PHONE ZOMBIES!

I guessed right about having trouble sleeping that week. Just falling asleep was hard enough. But then once I was out? My dreams were WEIRD.

There was this one really bad dream I had twice. I was up onstage in front of the whole school with no pants on. And when I went back to class, everybody started clowning on me, like, "You ain't got no pants on, fool!"

And I was all, "Man, shut up! I got pants on!"

But even while I was telling them that, I STILL didn't have pants on!

That messed with my head. I felt TERRIBLE when I woke up.

Then I had this other dream where I was at Tevin Bart's big old movie-star house, just chilling with him. Except there were these giant bears in his backyard! They were up on their hind legs, roaring at us while they banged on the glass door with their paws.

Tevin Bart was all, "Don't mind those bears. They can't eat you through the glass." But I freaked out and ran out his front door. Then the bears chased me down. I woke up in a sweat right before I got eaten.

It wasn't just the sleeping that was bad that week. I had trouble eating, too.

Well, not exactly eating. The eating part was fine. But what happened to the food after it got to my stomach was NOT. I spent a good bit of that week in the bathroom.

Probably best if I don't share the details.

Point is, I was pretty much a wreck by the time Thursday came around. Darren and Trish told us all we should look sharp for the showcase, so I wore my best shirt to school that day—the one with actual buttons up the front.

Soon as I got on the bus, Dewayne started clowning me for it.

"Is it school picture day?" he wanted to know.

But I was ready for him. I said, "It's Dewayne Pays Me Twenty Bucks Day! 'Cause I got a film premiering tonight that you bet me wasn't gonna happen. HOW 'BOUT THAT, PLAYA?"

It was perfect. Dewayne got this look like he'd just stepped in it.

But then J.R. ruined the whole thing.

"It ain't YOUR movie premiering!" he said. "It's Sierra's. Bet was for YOUR movie."

"That's coming soon!" I told him.

"Not yet, though."

I was a little mad at J.R. for that. But not too mad. 'Cause Dewayne's a deadbeat. He probably wasn't going to pay me that twenty bucks anyway.

Sitting still in class that whole day was HARD. It was so hard, I couldn't do it. But my teachers knew something was up, 'cause I was wearing a shirt with buttons. So they cut me slack.

After school ended, we had time to kill in film class, 'cause the showcase wasn't starting until six. I tried to get Sierra to show me the rough cut of *Toothpick*, but she didn't even have the footage at school. She'd uploaded everything we shot on day two to her computer at home. Then she took it off the camera before she returned it to

Darren. Reason being, she didn't want him knowing we'd shot that scene on the bus when he told us not to.

That turned out to be smart. 'Cause Darren was SO happy with us for not screwing anything up that when Trish left the room, he slid over to me and Sierra and dropped some AMAZING news.

"My boss wants me to work another double this weekend," he told us. "And I could REALLY use the money. Think you can handle shooting without me again? On the down low?"

"You got it!"

"Totally! We'll be super-careful! And not a word to Trish! Or anybody."

"Awesome." Darren gave us both fist bumps. "We'll do it just like last week. I'll drop the camera with you first thing Saturday morning, then pick it up the next day."

I just about had to bite my lip to keep from screaming. When he walked off, I turned to Sierra.

"You know what this means? We can shoot at the hospital!"

Instead of smiling back at me, she frowned.

"I don't know, M. That's shady."

"It's not! We'll be in and out!"

"We'll talk about it later," she said.

Then Trish came in with pizza that Afternoon Adventures had bought us for an early dinner, and we all chowed down.

After that, we headed to the showcase. They'd turned the main hallway of school into an art gallery. Kids, parents, and teachers were checking out all the stuff the kids had made after school over the past couple of months. Some of the kids in art class had drawn comics. When I saw those, I had a flashback to last spring's showcase. I'd put up some of my Toothpick panels, and they'd gone over pretty good.

I started to get a little sad about that. The movie stuff had taken up so much time that I hadn't drawn a Toothpick comic in forever, and I missed it.

But then I saw this display table that was all origami birds. And I felt a lot LESS bad about not being in art class.

Dad showed up while I was staring at the origami. I'd told him not to dress up. But he'd put on a tie anyway.

"That's some fine birds right there," he said. "Which one's yours?"

"Cut it out, Dad." I was too nervous for jokes.

Once everybody was done checking out the art, they brought us into the auditorium for the performances. There was all kinds of stuff on the program. Martial arts kids broke boards. A dance crew did a hip-hop routine. The musical theater class put on a whole Broadway song-and-dance. A couple of kids rapped. Amari played one of his music videos, and that went over great.

They even showed a clip from Jazmin's MeTube channel! And some of Khalid's stop-motion.

Trish had asked me if I wanted to show a scene from

the *Toothpick* movie. I'd said no, 'cause Sierra told me it wasn't edited yet. But watching everybody else's stuff, I started feeling left out. And I wished I could've gotten her to edit something in time to show it.

I was also getting nervous. Every time an act finished, I looked at the program and counted down to the *Phone Zombies* premiere. By the time we were three acts away, my stomach was flopping. I was getting worried I might barf up all the pizza.

Finally, it was time. Sierra got onstage with Darren and Trish to introduce the movie. Pretty much every kid in the room was in it as a zombie, so they were HYPED. The hooting and hollering was so loud, Darren and Trish had to shush the crowd a couple of times just to let Sierra get through the introduction.

She sounded even more nervous than I was. When she thanked Darren and Trish and the rest of us for all the hard work, her voice was shaking.

Then they got offstage, somebody turned down the lights, and the movie started.

It was REAL quiet at first. Almost TOO quiet.

And the first time I showed up on-screen, I could barely stand to watch. My head was six feet tall, and everybody was staring at it!

I squirmed in my chair, and Dad gave my arm a squeeze. I guess he was trying to be nice. But I yanked my arm away, 'cause it felt like pity. I didn't want that.

I was about to shut my eyes to the whole thing when
Giant Head Me cracked a joke.

The whole room blew up in a laugh.

A BIG laugh.

It was the best sound I'd ever heard in my life.

I'd had a room full of people laugh at me before—and
it did NOT feel good.

But this was different.

It was just like Sierra told me that day she dragged
me back to film class. When people are laughing WITH
you? And not AT you? Man, that's all the difference in
the world.

And the audience KEPT laughing. Not just at my stuff. Sierra got a TON of laughs. Jazmin got some, too. So did Khalid and Amari. Even the zombies were funny!

There was SO MUCH laughing! Dad sounded like he was going to choke from it!

There was too much laughing, to be honest. That crowd laughed so much, you couldn't hear a couple of the best jokes.

But that movie KILLED. When it was over, Dad gave me a big hug.

"You done good, son!" he told me. "That was the BOMB!"

This time, I didn't pull away from him.

Then everybody went out to the main hall and tore through a table full of cookies. And no joke—it was like I was a movie star! Parents and kids kept coming up to me with fist bumps and high fives and all kinds of *Great job!* and *That was dope!* and *You're FUNNY!*

They were even congratulating Dad!

I felt like a million dollars that night. At one point in the middle of it, I looked across the hall and saw Sierra getting mobbed by a crowd of folks all talking her up, too.

She caught my eye, and she gave me a smile.

And that smile just said *WE DID IT.*

When I got home that night, I couldn't sleep all over again.

All I could think was, if I could make *Toothpick Fights the Doom!* as good as *Phone Zombies* was, I might die from happiness. 'Cause my heart would just bust right open.

And we were close. Only one more day of shooting.

We were so close, I could taste it.

CHAPTER 21

ROUGH CUTS ARE ROUGH

"I can't believe we're still having this argument," Sierra muttered through her teeth.

We were sitting in the back of film class the next day. All those good vibes from *Phone Zombies* had lasted about five minutes.

'Cause Sierra was being a FOOL about the hospital scene.

She wanted to shoot the climax of the movie in a stupid PLAYGROUND!

"It'll be funny," she said.

"It ain't supposed to be funny!" I told her. "It's a SUPERHERO movie!"

"Superhero movies can be funny!"

"NOT THIS ONE!"

The whole room was staring at me. I tried to lower my voice.

"It's serious business," I told her. "Doom tryin' to KILL

that Angel! Toothpick gotta save her life! That ain't no playground stuff!"

Sierra shut her eyes and took a deep breath. Then she let it out real slow.

"Do you trust me?" she asked.

"I don't know!"

"Seriously? After last night? How'd *Phone Zombies* turn out?"

"Good."

"Better than good. Did you LIKE getting them laughs? All that applause? All those fist bumps?"

"Yeah. So?"

"So will you just TRUST ME that I know what I'm doing?"

"That was YOUR movie! *Toothpick*'s MY movie!"

"And you asked ME to direct it! 'Cause you trusted me! So TRUST ME when I say the climax is a HUNDRED times better in a playground."

I looked around to make sure Darren and Trish couldn't hear us.

"You just scared," I told her. "'Cause you think we'll get in trouble if we shoot in a hospital. But Tyrell said—"

"Tyrell been to jail!"

"It wasn't real jail! It was just juvie! And he's reformed now!"

Sierra rolled her eyes. "Not reformed enough."

"It's real simple," I told her. "A serious movie gotta have a serious climax. The hospital makes it serious."

"I don't think it's a—" She stopped in the middle of the sentence. Bunched her eyebrows up. Then shook her head.

"What?"

"Never mind."

"What? Say it!"

"I don't think this movie's as serious as you think it is," she told me.

"What's that supposed to mean?"

"It means—" She stopped herself again. "It's going to have a REAL specific tone. And you just gotta trust me it'll be good. If you could see the rough cut—"

"Then show it to me! Show me what you got!"

"I don't have it here," she said. "It's at home."

"So let's go to your place after this! Show me what you got."

"I don't think that's a good idea," Sierra told me. "Remember how up in your head you got when I showed you the *Phone Zombies* footage?"

"It won't be like that," I told her. "I got more experience now."

She thought about it. Then she shook her head again. "No. You should wait."

"Then I'll wait. Show me AFTER we shoot the hospital scene."

She let out a big sigh for about the fiftieth time.

"Fine. We'll go to my place after this. I'll show it to you."

Sierra's apartment was about ten blocks from mine. From the outside, the building looked the same kind of rundown. So did the stairs and the hallway inside.

But once we walked into her place, it was a whole other story. It was SPOTLESS in there. Kind of clean you only see in TV commercials.

It even SMELLED good. Like candy and soap.

The kitchen table had actual flowers! In a vase!

"Dang!" I said. "It's NICE in here."

"Don't touch anything," Sierra told me. "And take your shoes off. Mama likes it clean. She's a little uptight."

"Where she at?"

"She works late on Fridays."

There was a computer in the tiny living room. Sierra sat me down in front of it. "Now, remember," she told me. "Rough cuts are ROUGH. This ain't got music, or effects—"

"Just play it!" My heart was thumping.

This was IT. After all those years drawing Toothpick comics. All those weeks of work putting the movie together.

I was finally going to see Toothpick come to life!

Sierra pressed play.

And this was the stone-cold truth:

I HATED IT.

It started out okay. That battle in the Astral Plane, with me doing a voiceover while Sierra put a Len Burds effect over my drawings? That looked all right.

But then we got to the live-action scenes, and it went downhill FAST. When the Doom first showed up, Tyrell's Jordans were sticking out under his robe!

"WAIT!" I made Sierra pause the playback. "Look at that! His Jordans are showing!"

"It's good, though," she said.

"No it ain't! You gotta edit that out!"

"No, M. 'Cause the tone is—just keep watching."

I kept watching. And it kept getting worse. The whole thing was just SILLY. Like it was trying to be serious, but it

WASN'T. My voice sounded like a cartoon cricket. Sierra was playing Genie like a dope. And Jazmin as Angel was just plain bad. That girl could NOT act.

Then I saw myself turn into Toothpick for the first time.

And it made me want to cry.

Not in a good way.

I was trying to act all tough. But I was just this skinny little short kid! And my costume made me look even MORE skinny and short.

I was supposed to be strong and serious! A superhero!

But I just looked weak and stupid. Like a little kid.

Wearing ladies' fingernails.

I couldn't even watch the whole thing.

"Stop it!" I told Sierra. "Just turn it off."

"I told you, it's a real specific tone—"

"It's AWFUL! It's just DUMB!"

"No, dude! It's HILARIOUS."

"IT'S NOT SUPPOSED TO BE HILARIOUS!"

"That's WHY it's hilarious! It's funny 'cause it's serious!"

"That don't—no! NO!"

"Marcus, if you just take a step back and—"

"NO! You made it STUPID!"

"It's a GOOD stupid! It's FUNNY—"

"'Cause it's laughing at me! Not with me! AT ME!"

"That's not true! It's laughing WITH you!"

I had to get out of there. I was either going to scream or cry, and I did NOT want that girl seeing either one.

I ran for the door. She ran after me.

"Will you just trust me?"

"NO!"

I slammed the door on her so fast, I was halfway to the stairs before I realized I forgot my shoes.

Had to knock on her door to get them back.

That just made it worse. Like piling stupid on top of mad.

CHAPTER 22

LET'S GET THIS DONE!

I must've spent hours walking around the neighborhood before I finally cooled off.

I was SO ANGRY. That girl was ruining my movie! Trying to turn it into a joke!

I didn't know WHAT to do.

For a while, I thought about quitting.

But I couldn't. I'd come too far. Worked too hard!

And I could turn it around. Parts of what we shot were good. The opening. A couple of the early scenes.

Once I thought about it for a while, the only part that REALLY stunk was ME, when I was trying to be Toothpick.

I could reshoot that stuff. Maybe put some padding under my shirt so I looked ripped.

No. That'd look corny.

I could recast my part. So when Marko was Marko, it was me. But when he turned into Toothpick, it was a whole other actor.

A tall one. With muscles.

There was this kid, Jayden, a year above me in school. Played on the basketball team. He was long and lean. But we kinda looked the same in the face.

Maybe HE could play Toothpick. I could maybe even reshoot it so you never saw his face or something.

Eventually, I decided one way or another, I'd make it work.

But I had to get rid of Sierra. Never should've asked her to direct in the first place. She just wanted to clown it all up! Make everything a joke.

But I couldn't get rid of her yet. We had one more day of shooting to get through. I didn't want to mess that up. Especially the big fight scene at the hospital.

Couldn't get it done without Sierra. Darren wouldn't let me use the camera.

So I'd have to pretend it was cool between us. Get through that last day.

And maybe I could still make it work with me playing Toothpick. Maybe I wasn't that bad after all.

I just had to be better at it. TOUGHER. Ten times more FIERCE! Quit faking like I was a superhero and BE ONE!

If I couldn't get it done, I'd reshoot that stuff later. With Jayden or somebody else.

But the thing to do now was FINISH. Get it done. Then get all the footage back from Sierra. See what I could do with it myself.

Once I figured out the plan, I slept like a log that night.

First thing the next morning, all six of us—me, Sierra, Tyrell, Jazmin, Khalid, and Amari—met up outside Darren's building. I was there first. When Sierra showed, she tried to take me aside and smooth things over.

"Look, dude, I'm sorry if—"

"Don't even trip," I told her. "It's all good."

"You sure?"

"Totally. It's fine. I just went off a little yesterday."

"You sure?"

"Yeah. No worries. We're good."

"And you're with me on the whole tone thing?"

No, I am NOT was what I was thinking.

But I kept it to myself. Instead, I just shrugged. "We'll see how it goes."

I was proud of that. Old Me would've blown up at her. Even New Me was thinking, *I can't WAIT to fire your butt.*

But New Me kept my mouth shut. I was learning.

Tyrell rolled in last. Once we were all there, Sierra texted Darren. A minute later, he came out of his building, already dressed in his black-pants-white-shirt waiter outfit. He had the camera case in one hand and the audio case in the other.

"Where you shooting today?" he asked us.

Everybody just kind of looked at each other.

Then I said, "My place!"

"Just be careful," said Darren. "Don't get in trouble."

He handed over the equipment. Then he went back inside.

"Where we *actually* shooting?" Sierra asked.

"Follow me," said Tyrell. "It's round the way."

Tyrell led us to a street just a few blocks from Darren's. When we turned the corner and I saw the hospital, I stopped dead in my tracks.

There's a lot of hospitals in the city.

And until I laid eyes on it, I had no idea Tyrell was bringing us to THIS one.

The others got a few steps ahead before they realized I'd quit walking. One by one, they stopped and turned around.

"What's the matter, Marcus?" Khalid asked me.

I just kept staring at the building. My head was starting to spin.

"You okay?" Jazmin asked.

"Yeah. It's just . . . I've been here before."

"Is it okay?" Amari asked.

I shook off the dizziness. "It's PERFECT. Let's get this done!"

There was a Burger World across the street from the hospital. We sat down on one of the outside tables so Jazmin could help me glue my finger spears on.

"Can't you do this yourself?" she asked me. "All you gotta do is watch the video!"

"You're just better at it," I told her.

Amari was watching the entrance to the hospital. "So are we all going in at once? Seems like that'd make a scene."

"We'll stagger it," said Tyrell. "Me and Little Man will go in first. Find a room. Then text the room number to the rest of you. Then you come up in pairs. Long as you look like you know where you're going, nobody will get fussed."

Jazmin finished my nails. "Okay. You're good to go."

I stood up and looked at Tyrell. "Let's do it."

Before we could walk off, Sierra piped up.

"I'm out," she said.

"What?"

"I can't do this. It's shady." She shook her head. "Y'all want to shoot in there, I won't stop you. But I ain't going in. I'll wait out here."

The rest of us looked at each other.

Then Tyrell shrugged. "Suit yourself."

We crossed the street and went inside.

I knew right where I was going. It was like muscle memory. Past the front desk to the elevator. Straight up to three. I kept my hands balled into fists so people walking by couldn't see my finger spears.

"You sure?" Tyrell asked me when I pressed the button for the third floor.

I nodded. "Yeah. I know this place."

We got off on three. Just the sight of it started making my head spin again. But my feet knew where to go. Left off the elevator. Right at the nurses' station. Straight down to the end of the hall.

"Yo, Little Man!" Tyrell whispered. "Just passed an open room!"

"Hang on," I told him. I was headed for the last door on the left. Right beside the double exit door to the back stairs.

Room 301.

It was just like I remembered it.

Only this time, the bed was empty.

"Send a text," I told Tyrell. "This is where we're shooting."

CHAPTER 23

THE MOMENT I'D BEEN WAITING FOR

She lay on that bed like a helpless angel, her insides full of sickness.

Death was looming over her, all in black. Ready to steal that pure soul away.

I was off to one side, looking up at the scene.

It was like reliving a nightmare.

Only THIS time . . . I was gonna give it a happy ending.

I was going to stop that evil Death. Once and for all.

Crouching by the window, just out of frame, I realized something:

There was NO WAY I could recast this part.

This was MY FIGHT.

I HAD to be Toothpick.

I had to beat that Death down to NOTHING.

Khalid raised the camera, ready to film.

Amari held the microphone, high up on the boom.

Jazmin lifted her head from the pillow. Craned her neck around Tyrell to look at me.

"You want me to drool out that nasty grape jelly stuff now?"

"Get a mouthful of it," I told her. "But don't let it out till Khalid starts shooting."

Jazmin picked up the little water bottle we'd filled with fake Ooze. Took a swig, then set it down out of sight on the floor.

"*Mrrrfgrrfvrfffmrrwm!*" she grumbled through her clamped-down lips. Then she flopped her head back on the pillow.

"Action!" I told them.

Jazmin turned her head toward the window, staring off into space with a woozy death look as Khalid went in for a close-up.

Little by little, the Black Death Ooze leaked out her mouth.

The Doom reached for her throat with his big mean hands.

I sprang up!

Jumped forward!

Finger spears at the ready!

"NOT TODAY, DOOM!" I roared.

Then that stupid nurse busted in and wrecked everything.

"WHAT IN THE HECK IS GOING ON HERE?!"

There wasn't going to be a happy ending in room 301 after all.

It was just a different kind of nightmare.

Tyrell was the first one out. He banged through those double doors to the back stairwell and shot down the steps three at a time.

The rest of us followed him.

The whole way down, that nurse was barking at us from the third-floor landing.

"You can't be doing this! What's the matter with you! This is a HOSPITAL! Hey! I'm talking to you! HEY!"

I could still hear her yelling down the stairwell when I hit the ground floor on my way out.

CHAPTER 24

IT ALL FALLS APART

"What happened?" Sierra asked.

We were around the corner from the hospital, huffing and puffing in the parking lot of some bank. Sierra had followed us when we ran out the front door.

"We got busted," Amari told her.

"Naw, dawg," Tyrell grunted. "Busted is when they catch you. We got AWAY."

Sierra shook her head. "Not if they figure out it was us. Stuff could get REAL ugly."

"It won't," I said. "They don't know nothin' about us. We keep quiet, we'll be fine."

That's when Khalid started to moan.

"What's the matter?"

He held up the camera. "I left the case back in the room!"

My stomach dropped. I thought about it for a second.

"It ain't a problem!" I said. "We'll just get a new case."

Sierra glared at me. "Dude! Sticker on the case says

'PROPERTY OF AFTERNOON ADVENTURES!' And it's got the PHONE NUMBER!"

Now, THAT was a problem.

And there was only one way to solve it.

"Wait here," I said. Then I took off running, back toward the hospital.

I used the rear stairs instead of the elevator. I was hoping I could just duck in the room, grab the case, and run back out.

Good news was, room 301 was empty again. That nurse was gone.

Bad news was, the camera case was gone, too.

I didn't have a choice. I walked down the hallway toward the nurses' station.

Right back into the belly of the beast.

I could hear the nurses talking from halfway down the hall.

"Call the number," one of them was saying.

"Think I should?"

"Of course! These Adventures people need to know they can't be letting kids DO that!"

I was close enough to see them now. The nurse who busted us was standing with her back to me, talking to a second nurse who was sitting at the desk.

"You know, one of them looked like Angela's boy."

"Angela *Jenkins?* Our Angela?"

Just then, I saw the camera case. It was sitting on top of the counter, a couple of inches from the elbow of the nurse who had her back to me.

"Yeah. And you know, I think that was the *same* room—"

If I moved fast—

"HEY!"

I swiped the case off the counter and tore off, down the hall to the stairs.

"Come back here!" the first nurse yelled. But I wasn't stopping for nothing.

Last thing I heard as I busted through the door to the stairs was the second nurse's voice: "Was that boy wearing *acrylics?*"

The other kids were glad to see me holding the camera case.

But once I told them what I'd heard the nurses saying, it got DARK.

"They're going to kick us all out!" said Khalid. "I ain't never going to finish my stop-motion!"

"I'm gonna catch it if they call home over this," said Jazmin.

"Me too," Sierra told her. "But it's going to hit Darren the hardest. He wasn't supposed to let us take that equipment out of school. Probably lose his job over it."

I slumped down to sit on the curb. I felt lower than low.

I wanted to blame Khalid for leaving the case behind.

Or Tyrell, for having the idea to shoot wild at a hospital in the first place.

Or Sierra, for being a know-it-all and not trying harder to stop us.

But deep down, I knew the truth. This was on me.

A whole world of trouble was coming down on everybody's head. And it was my fault.

I wish I could say I figured out right there in the parking lot what I had to do to make it right. But I didn't. It took me a whole day of sitting with the guilt and the worry before I came up with my plan.

I was still working it out in my head when Dad came home from work Sunday night.

"So I got this phone call," he said.

Oh, man. I KNEW that couldn't be good.

"It was one of those nurses where your mama used to work. Told me this wild story about some kids showing up at the hospital yesterday. And first, I thought, 'That CAN'T be Marcus. 'Cause he ain't HALF that stupid.'"

"Naw, Dad," I told him. "I'm TWICE that stupid."

After I came clean and told him what I wanted to do to make it right, he didn't disagree.

Which was too bad. 'Cause I was hoping he'd try to stop me.

Monday morning, I showed up at school so early that when I got to the little Afternoon Adventures office next to the gym, Ms. Dorothy wasn't even there yet.

That was good. I needed to get to her before she checked her voice mail.

The saddest thing was, when she first saw me waiting outside her office door? She actually looked HAPPY to see me.

That woman had NEVER been happy to see me before.

"Marcus! The movie star! Who saved us all from the zombies! What can I do you for?"

"I got some bad news I gotta come clean about," I told her.

Once I started talking, Ms. Dorothy's smile went away fast.

I took the heat for the whole thing. Even some stuff I DIDN'T do, 'cause it was the only way to keep Darren out of it. I told her I'd snuck that camera equipment out the door Friday afternoon without him knowing a thing.

Then I told her none of the kids who were with me at the hospital went to our school. Said they were from across town. I'd met them online, in a movie chat. Didn't even know their last names. Couldn't track them down if you paid me.

I don't think Ms. Dorothy really believed it.

But believing it was a WHOLE lot easier for her than not believing it. 'Cause it meant all she had to do to solve the problem was kick me out of Afternoon Adventures.

Word spread fast. Sierra and the other kids tried to thank me, but I wouldn't hear it. I just wanted to forget about the whole thing.

That wasn't easy. The next morning when I got on the bus for school, Dewayne was waiting for me with a big old grin.

"I hear you owe me twenty bucks, playa! 'Cause you ain't NEVER making that movie now!"

He didn't tease me for long. I think I must've looked so heartbroken, even Dewayne felt bad for me.

CHAPTER 25

A LITTLE TALK IN A BIG GRAVEYARD

After I got kicked out of Afternoon Adventures, I didn't have it in me to do much of anything except mope around the apartment for a while.

Which was fine. 'Cause I couldn't have gone anywhere even if I wanted to. Dad said I was grounded as punishment for what happened. Had to stay in except when I was going to school and back.

The only good thing was that when I'd go home from school in the afternoon, I didn't have to look over my shoulder for Tyrell and his crew anymore. We weren't exactly tight, but I guess they respected me now. Or maybe they just felt sorry for me.

Nothing else was good about it. When Sierra and the other film kids saw me around, they'd say hi. But we mostly stopped talking. I think they felt bad about how things went down, and the easiest way to deal was just to pretend it never happened at all.

Sierra asked me on the bus once if I wanted to get all the movie footage back from her.

I said sure. But I didn't follow up. And neither did she.

Truth was, I didn't WANT that footage back. Watching it was just going to make me feel worse. What was I going to do with three-fourths of a movie? About a dumb kid who never had any business trying to be a superhero in the first place?

I was so torn up, I couldn't even draw Toothpick comics anymore. All they did was remind me of how bad I'd screwed up.

I did start drawing a new comic for a little while.

Called it *Darko Dummo: The Unluckiest Boy in the World.*
He'd walk down the street, and birds would poop on him.
Or air conditioners would fall out of windows and land
on his head.

But when I showed it to Dad, he got worried.

"This supposed to be funny?" he asked me. "Or sad?"

I just shrugged. "I don't know. Both?"

Then he wanted to know if I felt like talking to Ms.
Kimble, the school psychologist.

So I quit drawing Darko, 'cause I just didn't need the
hassle.

It was deep into November by then, and the weather
was starting to turn. One Saturday morning, Dad got up
early and looked out the window. It was gray and cold.

"Let's go visit your mama," he said.

Mom's resting place was this little plot deep in the middle
of the biggest cemetery in the city. The place was like
a maze, and her gravestone wasn't much bigger than a
shoebox. But we'd been there enough times that we could
find it without checking the directory.

On the way there, Dad bought fresh flowers from Mr.
Lee's deli. He gave me half, and we did our usual thing: said
a little prayer out loud together, then added our own private thoughts before we laid the flowers on her gravestone.

All I could think to say was *I'm sorry.*

Sorry I let you down, Mama. Sorry I messed up that hospital room. Sorry I got kicked out of after-school. Sorry I couldn't finish your movie.

I was crying a little by the time I finished.

Dad put his arm around me and gave my shoulder a squeeze.

"I messed it all up," I told him. "I was going to dedicate that movie to her, and I couldn't even get it finished."

"So finish it," he said.

"I can't! I got kicked out of film class!"

"So what? Since when you need a class to make a movie? Didn't need a class to make all those comics."

"A comic's just paper and pencil and pens. A movie needs a camera, and sound—"

"Ain't your phone got a camera?"

"That'd just look trash," I told him, even though I wasn't sure if it was true. "And my phone ain't got no battery left! Besides, I can't make the movie without the hospital scene."

"Why's that?"

"'Cause that's where Mama passed."

"Your movie was about Mama passing?"

"No. But yeah. Sort of. It's hard to explain."

"Give it a shot. I ain't got anywhere to be today."

"It was a Toothpick story. But, like, the whole way it got started . . . like, the comic . . . when I first drew it . . . was more, like, about . . ."

I stopped and took a deep breath. The air was cold in my lungs.

"Like, what if she DIDN'T pass? What if the cancer didn't get her? What if I could've stopped it? Y'know?"

Dad nodded. Gave my shoulder another squeeze.

"That's heavy stuff for a comedy."

"It wasn't a comedy!" I told him.

"Oh. Okay, then."

We were both quiet for a while after that. Finally, Dad put his flowers on the gravestone. I did the same. Then we stepped back to look at them.

"It's too bad, though," he said. "'Cause comedy's what

your mama loved. She got all the drama she needed at work. Being a nurse, she was knee-deep in it every day. When she came home at night, all she wanted was a bowl of ice cream and a good laugh. Like them Taylor Berry movies."

He chuckled to himself. "Or *Phone Zombies*! Your mama would've LOVED that movie. If she could've seen you in that, she would've been SO proud. Didn't I tell you that?"

I nodded. "About fifty times."

"It's the truth," Dad said. "Remember how you used to make her laugh? Boy, you could crack her up without even trying."

I remembered. And it made me happy even while it hurt. "She'd get those DEEP laughs. Belly laughs!"

"That's a gift," Dad told me. "Being able to make somebody laugh like that."

It took me a few seconds. But after Dad said that, what I needed to do was SO OBVIOUS! It was like it fell out of the sky and hit me on the head.

"Am I still grounded?" I asked Dad.

"Why? You got somewhere to go?"

"Yeah. I got a movie to finish."

CHAPTER 26

BACK IN BUSINESS!

Here's the thing I STILL can't believe about the *Toothpick* movie: that whole time I'd been trying to make it, I was totally, one thousand percent dead sure it HAD to end with the hospital scene.

And I was totally, one thousand percent dead WRONG.

Once I let go of that one scene? And I just let the story be whatever it needed to be? A whole TRUCKLOAD of ideas started hitting me!

There were a dozen ways to end that story. A hundred!

It was like I'd spent months beating my head against this brick wall, thinking I had to bust through it to get the movie made. But that whole time, all I needed to do was take a step back and just walk AROUND it. And there wasn't just one path around that brick wall. There were tons of them!

Not only that, but as soon as I took that step back, I could finally see what Sierra had been trying to tell me about the tone of it.

How did I EVER think scrawny little me playing a superhero was gonna be anything BUT funny?

I went straight from the cemetery to Sierra's place. I texted her on the way. But then my phone died like it always does. So I wasn't sure she'd gotten the message until I turned up the street and saw her waiting on her front stoop.

"What you all worked up about?" she wanted to know.

"We GOTTA finish the movie," I told her. "And it's GOTTA be a comedy."

A big old grin spread across her face. "So are you saying . . . I was RIGHT all along?"

"Not if you gonna get an attitude about it."

"What'll we do for a camera?" she asked. "'Cause I don't see Darren letting that equipment out of his sight again."

"We'll just use my phone," I told her.

She laughed out loud. "Marcus, your phone is a hundred years old! How you gonna shoot a movie on it when you can't even get texts?"

"I'll figure it out! I'll get a charger!"

She shook her head. "Uh-uh. No way."

I was fixing to give her a speech about how I had to make that movie NO MATTER WHAT.

But then she pulled her phone out of her jacket. "We'll use mine instead," she told me.

And that's what we did.

It wasn't easy. Making a movie is NEVER easy.

Especially when you're making it with somebody as bullheaded and bossy as Sierra. We fought like dogs just over how to rewrite the ending.

Then we had to get everybody back together for one more day of shooting. That was tough to schedule, 'cause basketball season had started for Jazmin. So she got busy.

Plus, she'd cut her hair again, and we had to figure out what to do with her head so we could shoot around it.

Then Tyrell had got himself in some kind of trouble, and for a couple of weeks, we couldn't even FIND the dude. Finally, he showed up again, and we scheduled the last day of shooting for a Saturday in mid-December.

But then the night before we were supposed to shoot? It snowed. EIGHT INCHES.

And there was just no way around that. We couldn't have two-thirds of a movie with no snow on the ground, and one-third of it looking like some winter wonderland.

Continuity-wise, that was about fifty times worse than Jazmin's hair.

For a while, I was thinking we'd have to wait until spring to finish.

And for the first time in my life, I started worrying about what I'd do if I actually GREW. What if I hit a growth spurt and was three inches taller by springtime?

That'd be a whole OTHER continuity problem.

But then the weather got screwy, and it went up to like sixty-five for a couple of days. That melted all the snow.

Then it was Christmas.

But then two days AFTER Christmas, we FINALLY got everybody together and shot the last of the movie.

I spent the rest of that Christmas week in Sierra's living room, arguing with her about how to do the edit while her mom yelled at me for getting potato chip crumbs on the floor.

Then—at 4:52 p.m. on New Year's Day—it was done.

I could hardly believe it.

It was DONE!

Toothpick Fights the Doom! was a MOVIE!

Fourteen minutes and thirty-six seconds of ACTUAL REAL LIVE MOVIE.

Sierra's mom was the first person we showed it to.

She liked it so much, she clapped when it was over. Then she saw the card I'd had Sierra put into the credits that read "DEDICATED TO THE MEMORY OF ANGELA JENKINS."

"Who's Angela Jenkins?" she asked me.

"That's my mom," I told her.

"Oh, bless your heart, baby," she said, and she gave me a hug.

I got a lump in my throat, but I didn't cry.

Then I went home and showed the movie to Dad.

And when that card came on the screen again, we BOTH cried.

"So now what?" he asked after we wiped our eyes.

"Now what, what?" I said. "It's done!"

"How you going to get it out there?" he asked me. "You gonna have a screening?"

"No, Dad," I told him. "That ain't how it works. We're gonna put it online. Upload it to MeTube. Then EVERYBODY can watch it. The whole world! It's gonna go viral!"

I was sure of that. Because anything THAT GOOD— that took THAT MUCH time and trouble to make—just HAD to get some eyeballs on it. It was a sure thing!

At least, that's what I thought.

CHAPTER 27

THE SECOND-HARDEST THING

By the time we finished *Toothpick Fights the Doom!*, I THOUGHT I'd learned all the lessons there were about moviemaking.

But I had one more left to learn. And this was it:

The HARDEST THING about a movie is making it.

But the SECOND-HARDEST THING is getting people to WATCH it.

If you ain't got a plan for that, it doesn't matter how good your movie is. It's just gonna sit there on MeTube like the ugly puppy at the back of the pet store. Peeing all over itself and chewing the bars on the cage while ten million people watch the cute puppy up front over and over again.

I didn't have a plan. So *Toothpick Fights the Doom!* was one ugly puppy.

After it had been out a week, it only had sixty-three views on MeTube!

And I was pretty sure fifty of those were me and the other kids in the cast rewatching it over and over.

The rest were probably my aunt Janice. 'Cause Dad sent her the link, and she kept emailing to tell me how great it was.

That felt a little good. But mostly, I was just crushed. 'Cause I'd let myself start dreaming about what'd happen when it went viral and everybody loved it. I figured the whole school would be giving me props like they did after the *Phone Zombies* screening.

And not just folks at school. Everybody! The whole world was gonna see it! They were gonna be begging for a sequel!

Then Capital Comics would call me up and want to make a deal for Toothpick! A twelve-issue run! Then a hundred more after that!

Then I started getting into roller-coaster-lunch-box fantasy territory. For a couple of days there, I was riding high on those dreams.

Which just made it hurt worse when nobody watched the movie. And I realized none of those dreams were gonna come true.

Then I got desperate. I posted links to the movie on every social media account I could think of. Started tagging everybody I knew, begging them to watch it.

I even got to begging folks I DIDN'T know. Like famous people. I tagged Taylor Berry. Tevin Bart. Bethany Maddish. About fifty other actors. A bunch of NBA players, 'cause J.R. told me that was a good idea.

Which it wasn't.

By the time *Toothpick Fights the Doom!* had been up on MeTube for a month, it still had only a couple of hundred views.

I crashed HARD over that.

Sierra tried to cheer me up. She was all, "*Phone Zombies* didn't get no love, either!"

Except *Phone Zombies* had around 1,800 views by then. That was NINE TIMES the love *Toothpick* was getting.

The comments section was all hype for it. But the numbers just weren't there. It only had like ten comments. And three of them were Aunt Janice. Which was just embarrassing.

So by the time February rolled around, I was starting to feel like a failure. Like the movie wasn't even that good after all.

Dad came home one night and found me curled up on the couch, feeling sorry for myself.

"It's like a tree falling in the forest, Dad! Nobody heard it! Didn't make a sound!"

"It's early yet."

"No, it ain't! It's been a month! And it ain't had a single new view in three days!"

"Gotta stop watching that counter, son. Gonna drive you out of your mind."

"Too late."

"It'll find an audience," he told me. "It's too good not to! Maybe not this month. But it'll always be there. Besides, it don't matter how many people see it! You did a hard thing, Marcus. And you did it WELL. You should hold your head up high."

"Just feels like such a comedown," I told him. "Like, with Sierra's movie—she got that big screening? Everybody pattin' her on the back. I didn't get NOTHING like that."

"I feel you," Dad said. "And maybe there's something we can do about it."

"Like what?"

"Gimme a minute," he said. "Right now, let's eat some dinner."

CHAPTER 28

THE SCREENING

Did I ever mention, I got the greatest dad in the world?

A couple of days after he found me moping on the couch, he came home with a sausage pizza and a big old smile.

"Remember my friend Lonnie?" he asked me.

"No."

"Sure you do. Tall brother with the goatee? Runs the community center? I play basketball with him on Saturdays?"

"Dad, I have no clue who that is."

"Well, you might want to find out. 'Cause you gonna owe him a solid."

"Why's that?"

"Like I said, he runs the community center. They got meeting rooms they rent out for gatherings and such. And Lonnie says he'll give me a break on the price for a room big enough to screen a movie in."

"What movie?" I asked. But my heart was already beating fast, 'cause I could see where this was going.

"YOUR movie!"

"We can screen *Toothpick*? At the community center?"

"That's what I'm saying! We'll do it on a Saturday night. Invite all the kids who worked on it. Get 'em to bring their friends."

"How many people can I invite?"

"As many as you want. Plus, the center's got a popcorn machine we can use."

"How much this going to cost?"

"Don't you worry. It's a birthday present."

"Dad, my birthday's in JULY."

"So it's an early one. Or it's late. Either way. What do you say?"

"Heck, yeah!"

That's how we wound up doing a cast-and-crew, friends-and-family screening of *Toothpick Fights the Doom!* at the North Side Community Center on a Saturday night in March.

I drew up a special invitation. Made it into a PDF, sent it out to all our relatives and everybody else I could think of.

Then the other kids in the movie invited everybody THEY knew.

YOU'RE INVITED TO
THE LIVE IN-PERSON PREMIERE
OF

TOOTH PICK
FIGHTS
THE DOOM!

PLUS SPECIAL MEET AND GREET
WITH THE CAST AND CREW OF
THE WORLD'S NEWEST & GREATEST
SUPERHERO MOVIE!
SATURDAY, MARCH 7
7:00PM
NORTH SIDE COMMUNITY CENTER
1126 KING BLVD
FREE POPCORN

And by the time we were done, we drew a CROWD. There must've been a hundred people there, easy. Including some folks you never would've guessed.

That nurse who kicked us out of the hospital room? Dad invited her! And she showed up! Name was Carol. Turned out she and my mom used to be tight. And she brought two more of mom's old friends from work.

Darren and Trish both came. That meant a lot. Especially 'cause I'm pretty sure Darren had to skip a waitering shift to be there.

Officer Shirley even came! And Ms. Dorothy from Afternoon Adventures! I still can't figure out who invited those two.

But they loved it.

EVERYBODY loved *Toothpick Fights the Doom!*

They loved it so much, we watched it twice in a row!

Then we showed *Phone Zombies*, just for the heck of it.

That went over great, too.

Afterward, we all hung out eating popcorn and drinking soda until the folks at the center booted us out 'cause they were closing down for the night.

It felt SO GOOD.

It was probably the best night of my life.

Not even probably. Definitely. Everybody congratulated me, Sierra, and the rest of the cast about fifty times.

Mom's old friends kept telling me how proud she would've been.

And Dewayne paid out our bet! Sort of. He came up to me at one point and said, "Playa, you EARNED this."

Then he slapped a twenty in my hand.

But it was Monopoly money.

"Man, what IS this?"

"You never said it had to be a REAL twenty bucks!"

"Don't eat no more of my popcorn, Dewayne. 'Cause that is just WEAK."

I wasn't really mad at him, though.

Nothing could've made me mad that night.

At some point in the middle of it, I realized Dad was right. It didn't matter how many people watched the movie on MeTube. I didn't make the movie for them.

I made it for ME.

And for US. The people in that room.

I worked HARD on that movie. We ALL did. Sierra, Jazmin, Khalid, Amari, and Tyrell and his crew.

We ALL worked our butts off. We made something AWESOME together.

And you know what?

That was enough. It was more than enough.

But the story wasn't quite over yet.

CHAPTER 29

WHAT'S NEXT?

When they closed up the community center, Tyrell was one of the last ones out the door. It was his first time seeing an audience watch him act, and he was FLYING. Just like I was when *Phone Zombies* premiered.

We got out to the sidewalk, and he grabbed me by the armpits. Lifted me right up off the ground.

"We gotta do a SEQUEL, Little Man!"

"That's a dope idea," I told him once he let me go. "We should do that."

Sierra and her mom were right behind us, close enough to hear everything. "Who's going to direct it?" Sierra asked.

I grinned at her. "Why you asking? You want the job?"

"I'd have to see a script first," she told me. "'Cause I don't sign on to just ANYTHING."

Dad laughed. "This girl got swagger!"

"You don't know the half of it," Sierra's mom told him.

We said goodbye to Tyrell and his crew. They headed the other way. Then Dad and I started up the street with Sierra and her mom. Parents up front, Sierra and me behind.

"Would you actually do another one?" she asked me.

"Maybe," I said. "I'm working on a new comic right now. Got to finish that first. Then we'll see. What about you? Got any other movies planned?"

"Man, I've ALWAYS got another movie planned."

"What's the next one? *Phone Zombies Two?*"

"No, it's an alien invasion thing. . . . But I don't want to talk about it. It's too soon."

"You writing a part for me?" I asked her.

She smirked. "Think I'd want to work with YOU again?"

I smirked right back. "Only if you want it to be GOOD."

We got to the end of the block. Dad and I were going left. Sierra and her mom were going right.

"All right, player," Sierra said. "We'll talk soon."

Then the weirdest thing happened: she hugged me.

And I'm pretty sure I hugged her back.

By the time Dad and I got home, I was wiped out. My cell phone was dead as usual. I plugged it in right before I got into bed.

The ringer was off, and just as I was halfway to passing out, I heard it buzz against the wood on the table where I left it. But I was too tired to get up and see who was texting me at that hour.

The next morning, I got up and brushed my teeth.

When I came back, my phone was buzzing again.

I picked it up and looked at the screen.

I had twenty-three new texts.

My screen was only showing the last two. They were both from Sierra:

THIS IS RIDICULOUS!!!

CALL ME NOW!!!!

I called her without even looking at the other twenty-some texts.

"What's up?" I said.

"THIS IS SO UNBELIEVABLE!" she yelled.

"What is?"

"Didn't you get my texts?"

"Yeah. But I didn't read them."

"Marcus! Tevin Bart shared *Toothpick*!"

"What?"

"He put the link on his ClickChat! And he said, 'This is the dopest thing ever!' Now EVERYBODY'S sharing it! Bethany Maddish! Little Doozy! Half the NBA!"

"Man, don't clown me! It's like eight in the morning!"

"I'm SERIOUS! It's blowing up!"

"Hang on."

I ran over to Dad's laptop. The MeTube page was bookmarked, so it only took a click to open it.

Last time I'd checked, *Toothpick Fights the Doom!* had 306 views.

Now it had 247,828.

Three seconds later, it was 248,101.

Then 248,724 . . .

249,583 . . .

I forgot I was still on the phone with Sierra until she screamed in my ear.

"WE'RE FAMOUS!"

KEVIN HART is an award-winning actor, comedian, and author. His films, including *Jumanji, Captain Underpants* and *The Secret Life of Pets*, have earned billions at the box office, and his stand-up comedy tours have sold out arenas and football stadiums, leading *Forbes* to name him the "king of comedy." *I Can't Make This Up*, his adult memoir, was a number one *New York Times* bestseller, remaining on the list for ten weeks straight. Kevin is also an entrepreneur, a television producer, and the chairman and CEO of HartBeat Productions. Inspiration for his debut middle-grade novel came from being told no when he was younger: *"No, you can't. No, you're not good enough. No, you don't have the right education or know the right people.* I'm stubborn, so I turned those *no*'s into fuel. Every time I heard one, it just made me work harder to prove wrong whoever said it." It is Kevin's hope that *Marcus Makes a Movie* will show kids that they are the only ones who can really say no to their goals: "If they can dream it, then they can do it." Kevin lives in Los Angeles with his family. He can be found on Twitter and Instagram at @KevinHart4Real.

GEOFF RODKEY is the author of the bestselling Tapper Twins comedy series; the Chronicles of Egg adventure trilogy; *We're Not from Here*, an NPR and *Kirkus* Best Book of the Year; and *The Story Pirates Present: Stuck in the Stone Age*, a comic novel bundled with a how-to guide for kids who want to create stories of their own. His first novel for adults, *Lights Out in Lincolnwood*, publishes in July. He's also the Emmy-nominated screenwriter of such films as *Daddy Day Care* and *RV*. Learn more at geoffrodkey.com, and follow Geoff on Twitter at @GeoffRodkey.

DAVID COOPER is a multimedia artist and muralist, born and raised in Brooklyn, New York. His work has appeared on book covers, ad campaigns, and editorial publications, such as the *New York Times*, *Print* magazine, and *POZ* magazine. He has painted large-scale murals at Miami Art Basel, Brooklyn, and has been exhibited at the New York Society of Illustrators. Learn more about David's work at davidcooperart.com.